Last Year at Marienbad

Text by
Alain Robbe-Grillet

for the film by
Alain Resnais

Translated by Richard Howard
Picture Editor: Robert Hughes

GROVE PRESS, INC.   NEW YORK

Also by Alain Robbe-Grillet:

THE VOYEUR
JEALOUSY
IN THE LABYRINTH

Last Year at Marienbad

Author: Original scenario and dialogue by Alain Robbe-Grillet
Director: Alain Resnais
Producers: Pierre Courau (Précitel)
          Raymond Froment (Terrafilm)
Starring: Delphine Seyrig, Giorgio Albertazzi, Sacha Pitoeff
With: Mmes. Françoise Bertin, Luce Garcia-Ville, Héléna Kornel, François Spira, Karin Toeche-Mittler, and Messrs. Pierre Barbaud, Wilhem von Deek, Jean Lanier, Gerard Lorin, Davide Montemuri, Gilles Queant, Gabriel Werner
Assistant to Mr. Resnais: Jean Léon
Director of Photography: Sacha Vierny
Cameraman: Philippe Brun
Settings: Jacques Saulnier
Sound Engineer: Guy Villette
Editing: Henri Colpi and Jasmine Chasney
Music: Francis Seyrig

The shooting of the exteriors and natural settings for the film was done at Munich (the Châteaux of Nymphenburg, Schleissheim, etc.); interiors: Studios Photosonor, Paris.
Script girl: Sylvette Baudrot

The film lasts one hour and thirty-three minutes.

The publishers would like to express their appreciation for the help and cooperation given by the French Film Office and by the American film distributors of *Last Year at Marienbad,* Astor Pictures, Inc., and especially to Mr. Joseph G. Besch.

5

Alain Robbe-Grillet

Alain Resnais

Introduction

ALAIN RESNAIS AND I ARE often asked how we worked together on the conception, writing and shooting of this film. Merely answering this question will provide a whole point of view with regard to cinematic expression.

The collaboration between a director and his script writer can take a wide variety of forms. One might almost say that there are as many different methods of work as there are films. Yet the one that seems most frequent in the traditional commercial cinema involves a more or less radical separation of scenario and image, story and style; in short, "content" and "form."

For instance, the author describes a conversation between two characters, providing the words they speak and a few details about the setting; if he is more precise, he specifies their gestures or facial expressions, but it is always the director who subsequently decides how the episode will be photographed, if the characters will be seen from a distance or if their faces will fill the whole screen, what movements the camera will make, how the scene will be cut, etc. Yet the scene as the audience sees it will assume quite different, sometimes even contradictory meanings, depending on whether the characters are looking toward the camera or away from it, or whether the shots cut back and forth between their faces in rapid succession. The camera may also concentrate on something entirely different during their conversation, perhaps merely the setting around them: the walls of the room they are in, the streets where they are walking, the waves that break in front of them. At its extreme, this method produces a scene whose words and gestures are quite ordinary and unmemorable, compared to the forms and movement of the image, which alone has any importance, which alone appears to have a meaning.

This is precisely what makes the cinema an art: it creates a reality with forms. It is in its form that we must look for its true content. The same is true of any work of art, of a novel, for instance: the choice of a narrative style, of a grammatical tense,

7

of a rhythm of phrasing, of a vocabulary carries more weight than the actual story. What novelist worthy of the name would be satisfied to hand his story over to a "phraseologist" who would write out the final version of the text for the reader? The initial idea for a novel involves both the story and its style; often the latter actually comes first in the author's mind, as a painter may conceive of a canvas entirely in terms of vertical lines before deciding to depict a skyscraper group.

And no doubt the same is true for a film: conceiving of a screen story, it seems to me, would mean already conceiving of it in images, with all the detail this involves, not only with regard to gestures and settings, but to the camera's position and movement, as well as to the sequence of shots in editing. Alain Resnais and I were able to collaborate only because we saw the film in the same way from the start; and not just in the same general way, but exactly, in the construction of the least detail as in its total architecture. What I wrote might have been what was already in his mind; what he added during the shooting was what I might have written.

It is important to stress this point, for so complete an understanding is probably quite rare. But it is precisely this understanding that convinced us to work together, or rather to work on a common project, for paradoxically enough, and thanks to this perfect identity of our conceptions, we almost always worked separately.

Initially, it was the producers who had the notion of bringing us together. One day late in the winter of 1959-60, Pierre Courau and Raymond Froment asked me if I would like to meet Resnais, with the idea of eventually writing for him. I immediately agreed to the meeting. I knew Resnais' work and admired the uncompromising rigor of its composition. In it I recognized my own efforts toward a somewhat ritual deliberation, a certain slowness, a sense of the theatrical, even that occasional rigidity of attitude, that hieratic quality in gesture, word and setting which suggests both a statue and an opera. Lastly, I saw Resnais' work as an attempt to construct a purely mental space and time—those of dreams, perhaps, or of memory, those of any affective life—without worrying too much about the traditional relations of cause and effect, or about an absolute time sequence in the narrative.

Everyone knows the linear plots of the old-fashioned cinema, which never spare us a link in the chain of all-too-expected events: the telephone rings, a man picks up the receiver, then we see the man on the other end of the line, the first man says he's coming, hangs up, walks out the door, down the stairs, gets into his car, drives through the streets, parks his car in front of a building, goes in, climbs the stairs, rings the bell, someone opens the door, etc. In reality, our mind goes faster—or sometimes slower. Its style is more varied, richer and less reassuring: it skips certain passages, it preserves an exact record of certain "unimportant" details, it repeats and doubles back on itself. And this *mental time,* with its peculiarities, its gaps, its obsessions, its obscure areas, is the one that interests us since it is the tempo of our emotions, of our *life.*

These were the things Resnais and I talked about during our first meeting. And we agreed about *everything.* The following week, I submitted four script projects; he said he would be willing to shoot all four, as well as at least two of my novels. After thinking it over a few days, we decided to begin with *Last Year at Marienbad,* as it was already called (or sometimes only *Last Year*).

Then I began to write, by myself, not a "story" but a direct shooting script, in other words a shot-by-shot description of the film as I saw it in my mind, with, of course, the corresponding dialogue and sound. Resnais came regularly to look at the text and make sure that everything was going as he imagined it himself. Once this writing was finished we had a long series of discussions, which again confirmed our complete agreement. Resnais understood so perfectly what I wanted to do that the few changes he suggested—at certain points in the dialogue, for instance—always followed my own intention, as if I made notations on my own text.

The actual shooting proceeded in the same way: Resnais worked alone—that is, with the actors and with Sacha Vierny, the director of photography, but without me. I never even set foot on the set, for I was in Brest and then in Turkey while they were shooting in Bavaria and later in the Paris studio. Resnais has written elsewhere about the strange atmosphere of those weeks, in the icy châteaux of Nymphenburg, in the frozen park of Schleissheim, and about the way Giorgio Albertazzi, Delphine Seyrig and Sacha Pitoeff gradually identified themselves with our three nameless characters who had no past, no links among themselves except those they created by their own gestures and voices, their own presence, their own imagination.

When I returned to France and finally saw the film, it was already at the rough-cut stage, having already virtually achieved its form; and that form was indeed the one I had wanted. Resnais had kept as close as possible to the shots, the setups, the camera movements I suggested, not on principle but because he felt them in the same way I did; and it was also because he felt them in the same way that he had changed them when it was necessary. But of course he had in every case done much more than merely respect my suggestions: he had carried them out, he had given everything in the film existence, weight, the power to impose itself on the spectator's senses. And then I understood everything he had put in himself (though he kept insisting he had merely "simplified"), everything that was not mentioned in the script and that he had had to invent, in each shot, to produce the strongest, most convincing effect.

All that remained for me to do was complete a few transition passages in the text, while Henri Colpi added the finishing touches to the editing. And now I can point to no more than one or two places in the whole film where perhaps . . . : here a caress I saw as less explicit, there a mad scene that could have been a little more spectacular. . . . But I mention these trifles only for conscience's sake, since we had even intended, at the end, to sign the completed film jointly, without separating scenario from direction in the credits.

But wasn't the story itself already a kind of *direction* of reality? A brief synopsis is enough to show the impossibility of using it as the basis for a film in traditional form, I mean a linear narrative with "logical" developments. The whole film, as a matter of fact, is the story of a persuasion: it deals with a reality which the hero creates out of his own vision, out of his own words. And if his persistence, his secret conviction, finally prevail, they do so among a perfect labyrinth of false trails, variants, failures and repetitions!

This takes place in an enormous hotel, a kind of international palace, huge, baroque, opulent but icy: a universe of marble and stucco, columns, moldings, gilded ceilings, statues, motionless servants. Here the anonymous, polite, no doubt rich, idle guests observe—seriously though without passion—the strict rules of their games (cards, dominoes . . .), their ballroom dances, their empty chatter, or their marksmanship contests. In this sealed, stifling world, men and things alike seem victims of some spell, as in the kind of dreams where one feels guided by some fatal inevitability, where it would be as futile as to try to change the slightest detail as to run away.

A stranger wanders from one salon to another—alternately full of elegant guests, or empty—opens doors, bumps into mirrors, follows endless corridors. His ears register snatches of phrases, chance words. His eyes shift from one nameless face to another. But he keeps returning to the face of a young woman, a beautiful perhaps still living prisoner of this golden cage. And so he offers her the impossible, what seems most impossible in this labyrinth where time is apparently abolished: he offers her a past, a future and freedom. He tells her that he and she have already met the year before, that they had fallen in love, that he has now come to a rendezvous she herself had arranged, and that he is going to take her away with him.

Is the stranger a mere seducer? Is he a madman? Or is he simply confusing two faces? The young woman, in any case, begins by treating the situation as a joke, a game like any other, intended merely to amuse. But the man is not laughing. Stubborn, serious, convinced of this past meeting that he gradually records, he insists, offers proof. . . . And the young woman, little by little, almost reluctantly, gives ground. Then she grows frightened. She draws back. She doesn't want to leave this false but reassuring world of hers which she is used to and which is symbolized for her by another man, solicitous, disillusioned and remote, who watches over her and who may in fact be her husband. But the story the stranger is telling assumes ever greater reality, becomes more and more coherent, increasingly present and irresistibly true. Present and past, finally, are intermingled, while the growing tension between the three protagonists creates fantasies of tragedy in the heroine's mind: rape, murder, suicide. . . .

11

Then, suddenly, she is ready to yield.... She already has yielded, in fact, long since. After a final attempt to resist, to offer her guardian a last chance of winning her back, she seems to accept the identity the stranger offers her, and agrees to go with him toward something, something unnamed, something *other*: love, poetry, freedom... or maybe death....

Since none of these three characters has a name, they are represented in the script by simple initials, for the sake of convenience alone. The man who is perhaps the husband (Pitoeff) is designated by the letter M, the heroine (Seyrig) by an A, and the stranger (Albertazzi) by the letter X, of course. We know absolutely nothing about them, nothing about their lives. They are nothing but what we see them as: guests in a huge resort hotel, cut off from the outside world as effectively as if they were in a prison. What do they do when they are elsewhere? We are tempted to answer: nothing! Elsewhere, they don't exist. As for the past the hero introduces by force into this sealed, empty world, we sense he is making it up as he goes along. There is no last year, and Marienbad is no longer to be found on any map. This past, too, has no reality beyond the moment it is evoked with sufficient force; and when it finally triumphs, it has merely become the present, as if it had never ceased to be so.

No doubt the cinema is the preordained means of expression for a story of this kind. The essential characteristic of the image is its presentness. Whereas literature has a whole gamut of grammatical tenses which makes it possible to narrate events in relation to each other, one might say that on the screen verbs are always in the present tense (which is what is so strange, so artificial about the "novelized films" which have been restored to the past tense so dear to the traditional novel!): by its nature, what we see on the screen *is in the act of happening*, we are given the gesture itself, not an account of it.

Yet the most narrow-minded spectator has no difficulty understanding the flashback; a few blurry seconds, for instance, are enough to warn him of a shift to memory: he understands that from this point on he is watching an action in the past, and the sharp focus can then be resumed for the remainder of the scene without his being disturbed by an image which is really indistinguishable from the present action, an image which is in fact *in the present tense*.

Having granted memory, the spectator can also readily grant the imaginary, nor do we hear protests, even in neighborhood movie theaters, against those courtroom scenes in a detective story when we *see* a hypothesis concerning the circumstances of a crime, a hypothesis that can just as well be false as true, made mentally or verbally by the examining magistrate; and we then see, in the same way, during the testimony of various witnesses, some of whom are lying, other fragments of scenes that are more or less contradictory, more or less likely, but which are all presented with the same kind of image, the same realism, the same presentness, the same objectivity. And this is equally true if we are shown a scene in the future imagined by one of the characters, etc.

What are these images, actually? They are imaginings; an imagining, if it is vivid enough, is always in the present. The memories one "sees again," the remote places, the future meetings, or even the episodes of the past we each mentally rearrange to suit our convenience are something like an interior film continually projected in our own minds, as soon as we stop paying attention to what is happening around us. But at other moments, on the contrary, all our senses are registering this exterior world that is certainly there. Hence the total cinema of our mind admits both in alternation and to the same degree the present fragments of reality proposed by sight and hearing, and past fragments, or future fragments, or fragments that are completely phantasmagoric.

And what happens when two people are exchanging remarks? Take this simple dialogue:

"What if we went to some beach? A huge, empty beach where we'd lie in the sun. . . ."

"With the weather we're having? We'd spend the day inside, waiting for the rain to stop!"

"Then we'd make a wood fire in the big fireplace. . . ." etc.

The street or the room where they are has disappeared from the minds of the speakers, replaced by the images each suggests. There is actually an *exchange of views* between them: the long strip of sand where they are lying, the rain streaming across the panes, the dancing flames. And the cinema audience would cer-

13

tainly have no difficulty understanding if what was shown was not the street or the room, but instead—and while listening to the dialogue—the couple lying on the sand in the sun, then the rain falling and the characters taking shelter in the house, then the man, as soon as they are inside, arranging the logs on the hearth. . . .

In this context, it is apparent what the images of *Last Year at Marienbad* might be, since the film is in fact the story of a communication between two people, a man and a woman, one making a suggestion, the other resisting, and the two finally united, as if that was how it had always been.

Hence the movie audience seemed to us already well prepared for this kind of story by its acceptance of such devices as the flashback and the objectivized hypothesis. It will be said that the spectator risks getting lost if he is not occasionally given the "explanations" that permit him to locate each scene in its chronological place and at its level of objective reality. But we have decided to trust the spectator, to allow him, from start to finish, to come to terms with pure subjectivities. Two attitudes are then possible: either the spectator will try to reconstitute some "Cartesian" schema—the most linear, the most rational he can devise—and this spectator will certainly find the film difficult, if not incomprehensible; or else the spectator will let himself be carried along by the extraordinary images in front of him, by the actors' voices, by the sound track, by the music, by the rhythm of the cutting, by the passion of the characters . . . and to this spectator the film will seem the "easiest" he has ever seen: a film addressed exclusively to his sensibility, to his faculties of sight, hearing, feeling. The story told will seem the most realistic, the truest, the one that best corresponds to his daily emotional life, as soon as he agrees to abandon ready-made ideas, psychological analysis, more or less clumsy systems of interpretation which machine-made fiction or films grind out for him *ad nauseam,* and which are the worst kinds of abstractions.

The text that follows is in principle the one given to Resnais before the shooting began, made somewhat more accessible by a slightly different presentation (sound and image, for instance, originally on separate pages). But even at that stage we had anticipated that certain passages of the offscreen narrative (that is, spoken by the voice of a character not on the screen) should be changed or enlarged during the editing, in consideration of the final image (to obtain a precise correspondence of content or duration); these few phrases have therefore been replaced in the original text.

The attentive spectator will naturally notice discrepancies between this account of a film and the actual film as seen. These slight changes have either been dictated by material considerations, such as the architectural arrangement of the settings used, even sometimes by a simple concern for economy, or else imposed on the director by his own sensibility. But it is not to dissociate myself from Alain Resnais' mediations that I present my initial text here, for on the contrary that text has only been reinforced, as I have indicated above; the only reason is one of probity, since the text is published under my signature alone.

The reader will find few technical terms in these pages, and perhaps the indications for editing, set-up shots and camera movements will make the specialist smile. This is because I was not a specialist myself, and because I was writing a shooting script for the first time. I hope that in any case this factor will make reading the scenario less tedious for a larger public.

A. R.-G.

OPENING WITH A ROMANTIC, PASSIONATE, violent burst of music, the kind used at the end of films with powerfully emotional climaxes (a large orchestra of strings, woodwinds, brasses, etc.), the credits are initially of a classical type: the names in fairly simple letters, black against a gray background, or white against a gray background; the names or groups of names are framed with simple lines. These frames follow each other at a normal, even rather slow, rhythm.

Then the frames are gradually transformed, grow broader, are embellished with various curlicues which finally constitute a kind of picture frame, at first flat, then painted in *trompe-l'oeil* so as to appear to be three dimensional.

Finally, in the last credits, the frames are real, complex and covered with ornaments. At the same time, the margin around them has widened slightly, revealing a little of the wall where these pictures are hung, the wall itself decorated with gilded moldings and carved woodwork.

The last two credit titles, instead of constituting separate shots, are gradually revealed by a lateral movement of the camera which, without stopping on the first frame when it is centered, continues its slow, regular movement, passes across a section of the wall containing only woodwork, gilding, molding, etc., then reaches the last frame, containing the last name or names of the credits, which could begin by less important names and end with the major ones, or even mix them, especially toward the end. This last picture has a considerable margin of wall around it, as if it were seen from farther away. The camera passes across this without stopping, then continues its movement along the wall.

Parallel to the development of the image during the credits, the music has gradually been transformed into a man's voice— slow, warm, fairly loud but with a certain neutral quality at the same time: a fine theatrical voice, rhythmical but without any particular emotion.

This voice speaks continuously, but although the music has stopped completely, we cannot yet understand the words (or in any case we understand them only with the greatest difficulty) because of a strong reverberation or some effect of the same sort (two identical sound tracks staggered, gradually superimposing until the voice becomes a normal one).

X's VOICE: *Once again—[1] I walk on, once again, down these corridors, through these halls, these galleries, in this structure—of another century, this enormous, luxurious, baroque, lugubrious hotel—where corridors succeed endless corridors—silent deserted corridors overloaded with a dim, cold ornamentation of woodwork, stucco, moldings, marble, black mirrors, dark paintings, columns, heavy hangings—sculptured door frames, series of doorways, galleries—transverse corridors that open in turn on empty salons, rooms overloaded with an ornamentation from another century, silent halls. . . .*

Beginning at the end of the credits, the camera continues its slow, straight, uniform movement down a sort of gallery of which only one side is seen, fairly dark, lit only by regularly spaced windows on the other side. There is no sunshine, it may even be twilight. But the electric lights are not on; at regular intervals, a lighter area, opposite each invisible window, shows more distinctly the moldings that cover the wall.

---

[1] The dash represents a slight pause, more emphatic than the meaning of the text suggests.

The field of the image includes the entire wall, from top to bottom, with a thin strip of the floor or the ceiling, or both. The shot is not taken from directly opposite the wall, but at a slight angle (toward the direction in which the camera advances).

The wall thus revealed, regularly explored yard by yard, is the same wall as that already glimpsed between the two last picture-frames of the credits: that is, a surface decorated by a profusion of baguettes, ogees, friezes, cornices, brackets and stucco embellishments of all kinds.

Moreover the panels are occupied by framed paintings, all placed at eye level. We find here mainly old-style prints showing a garden *à la française* with geometric lawns, shrubbery clipped into cones, pyramids, etc., gravel walks, stone balustrades, statues on massive cubical pedestals, their attitudes stiff and rather em-

phatic; some photographs of the hotel itself, and in particular of the corridor-gallery where we are (showing, for instance, the diminishing perspective of the two walls). Lastly, a theater poster (also framed) for a play with a foreign, meaningless title, the rest of the poster illegible except perhaps for a line in larger letters: *Tonight only. . .*

The corridor-gallery may include columns and pilasters, lateral doors that are closed and doorways opening down long transverse corridors, or even onto halls and lobbies.

The entire setting is empty. Only occasionally, perhaps, at the corner of a hall or at the far end of a transverse corridor, a motionless, frozen servant in elaborate livery, or else a statue (but without a pedestal).

If a straight trajectory of this length is impossible, it can be replaced by a labyrinthine series of corridors and salons, giving the same impression of a slow, continuous, virtually unending passage.

During all this time, the same neutral and monotonous voice will continue speaking the text. The words, by the end of the credits, have become normally comprehensible.

X's VOICE: . . . *where the sound of advancing footsteps is absorbed by carpets so thick and heavy that nothing can be heard, as if the ear of the man walking on once again, down these corridors —through these halls, these galleries, in this structure of another century, this enormous, luxurious, baroque, lugubrious hotel— where endless corridors succeed silent, deserted corridors— overloaded with a dark and cold ornamentation of woodwork, stucco, moldings—marble, black mirrors, dark paintings, columns, heavy hangings—sculptured door frames, series of doorways, galleries, transverse corridors—that open in turn on empty salons, overloaded with an ornamentation from another century—silent halls where the sound of footsteps is absorbed by carpets so heavy, so thick that nothing reaches the ear—as if the ear itself were very far away, very far away from the floor, from the carpets, very far away from this heavy and empty setting, very far away from this complicated frieze that runs just under the ceiling, with its branches and its garlands, like dead leaves, as if the floor were still sand or gravel. . . .*

20

The images that accompany this text do not correspond exactly with the elements of the setting to which it refers. But the photography must have a constant character which is maintained, moreover, during the entire film: a distinct and brilliant image, even in the darker sections, giving everything a kind of varnished quality.

From the beginning, the camera has not stopped at any particular point, moving on without lingering over the more significant images (the garden). The latter, moreover, are not always very well lit, not being necessarily located opposite one of the windows that succeed each other at fixed intervals (the distances are constant and the tempo the same) on the other (still invisible) side of the gallery.

At the end of this gallery there is a door, or even a series of

doors (as monumental as possible) that the camera passes through with the same continuous movement maintained since the end of the credits. Here too the ornamentation must be heavy, complicated, rather lugubrious. There may be columns, steps, porticoes. At the same time, the darkness becomes more intense, though not producing a gray image; on the contrary, there are some extremely clear details (highlights of capitals, of various moldings) seen against an equally distinct darkness, without its being apparent what source of light is responsible for these strange effects.

Finally a dark salon is seen, really very dark this time, where a light (vague at first, but gradually becoming distinct as the camera draws closer) is emanating from precisely the direction toward which the image is advancing. The salon is a kind of theater, but not arranged in the customary manner: there are chairs and armchairs arranged in groups of varying size, merely turned in the same direction. All the seats are occupied: many men in evening clothes, and a few women, also very elegantly dressed. The faces are seen in profile or in three quarters from behind, lit from in front by the light coming from the stage. All the bodies are quite motionless, the faces absolutely set, the eyes fixed. The light grows brighter toward the front rows, but the room retains its character of a theater where the faces are illuminated by the very spectacle they are watching.

The offscreen text continues, without interruption, as the camera enters the room, then while the heads of the spectators file past. The tone becomes less neutral, more "expressive."

X's voice: . . . *or stone slabs, on which I advanced, as though to meet you—between these walls covered with woodwork, stucco, moldings, pictures, framed prints, among which I was walking—among which I was already waiting for you, very far away from this setting where I now stand, in front of you, still waiting for the man who will no longer come, who no longer threatens to come, to separate us again, to tear you away from me.* (A pause.) *Are you coming?*

After a silence, it is a woman's voice (the woman is also invisible on the screen) that answers, in the same rather theatrical tone, but still measured, calm, cadenced. A beautiful, deep voice, but

restrained; it is the voice of the actress who will be seen shortly afterward.

ACTRESS' VOICE: *We must still wait—a few minutes—more—no more than a few minutes, a few seconds . . .* (A silence.)

The man's voice resumes, speaking the text more and more theatrically, as though on a stage.

X's VOICE: *A few seconds more, as if you yourself were still hesitating before separating from him—from yourself—as if his silhouette, though already gray, already paler, still threatened to reappear—in this same place where you had imagined it with too much force—too much fear, or hope, in your fear of suddenly losing this faithful link with . . .*

The voice has gradually slowed, then stopped, suspended. And the actress' voice answers it, after a short silence.

ACTRESS' VOICE: *No, this hope—this hope is now without any object. This fear of losing such a link, such a prison, such a lie has passed.—This whole story is already over now. It came to an end—a few seconds . . .*

Having reached the first row of spectators, the camera continues its movement, passing in review, from almost directly in front now, the faces aligned, frozen with attention, and brightly illuminated by the light from the stage. But the camera's speed has gradually decreased and the image finally comes to rest on a few motionless heads.

Then the shot cuts abruptly to the stage itself, brilliantly lit and occupying the entire screen.

The stage represents a garden *à la française* (or *à l'italienne*), recalling the prints glimpsed in the corridor, in fact copied exactly from one of them. A kind of graveled terrace with a stone balustrade at the back (overlooking the invisible lawns), a statue at one side (on a cubical pedestal, one or two antique-looking figures whose grandiloquent postures seem to signify something, but what?) and on the other a portico or some columns, or the beginning of a pergola, a doorway through which someone might appear.

Two actors are on the stage, a woman between twenty-five and thirty, a man between thirty-five and forty, in formal dress of the last century. They are both facing the doorway described above. The man is slightly upstage in relation to the woman. He is seen in profile, she in three-quarters from behind.

The actress finishes the sentence which her voice had begun offscreen at the end of the preceding shot.

THE ACTRESS: *. . . more—it has come to a close. . . .*

It is the actor, on the stage, who answers her, and no longer X's voice, which has been heard since the beginning of the film.

THE ACTOR: *. . . forever—in a past of marble, like these statues, this garden carved out of stone—this hotel itself with its halls deserted now, its motionless, mute servants long since dead no*

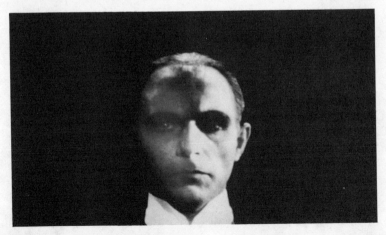

doubt, who still stand guard at the corners of the corridors, along the galleries, in the deserted salons, through which I walked to meet you, at the thresholds of the doors thrown wide that I walked through one after the other to meet you, as if I were passing between two hedges of motionless faces, frozen, watchful, indifferent, while I was already waiting for you, forever, and while I am still waiting for you as you still hesitate perhaps, still staring at the door to this garden....

The actor and the actress have remained motionless since their appearance on the screen. They say nothing now, still not moving, and the silence lasts for quite a long time, until the sound of a clock chiming the hour (several clear, regularly spaced strokes) breaks the pose: the man remaining frozen, the woman turns around, not toward him but toward the public (that is, toward the camera) to answer.

THE ACTRESS: *Very well.* (Then, after a pause, but without making the slightest gesture toward the man:) *Now I am yours.*

During the burst of applause from the (invisible) audience, the curtain falls. The two actors remain in the same position, without bowing. The curtain rises and falls twice more during the applause without the actors making a single gesture. The woman's

attitude should be quite particularized here, like that of a statue: a certain position of the arm which raises her hand to the hollow of her shoulder, a gesture readily recognizable when it recurs. The applause continues, very violent, very heavy, quite long; then gradually transforming itself into music identical to that heard at the beginning of the credits (very "end of a tearjerker") whose intensity rapidly increases until it drowns out the applause, which fades out altogether while the curtain falls for the last time. And the shot changes.

Reverse angle: the theater, now brightly lit. The applause is over, the specators have stood up. They have formed groups here and there (the chairs not occupying the entire room). The camera makes a more or less circular movement through the groups. A few characters are still facing the (invisible) stage, no longer applauding, but still staring straight ahead, standing motionless, as though under the spell of the spectacle which has just concluded. These people are generally isolated; but others in the same position are also to be found within certain groups, which thereby assume a rather strange quality: a part of their constituents (one or two) not facing the center of the circle. The violent and impassioned music continues with the same force, completely drowning out the sound of the conversations.

The camera comes to a stop on a woman standing apart, twenty-five to thirty years old, beautiful but somehow empty (we shall refer to her by the letter A), quite tall, statuesque. She is seen in precisely the position the actress on the stage had taken as the curtain fell. But the camera does not hold this stationary shot long.

A series of stationary shots follows, showing the groups already seen before. The postures of the characters have not changed, or have changed only slightly. Some faces are still turned toward the invisible stage. The discussions are occasionally animated but always polite (and nothing can be heard because of the music). A few gestures, significant but incomprehensible (out of context), and also perfectly polite. This series of shots must be shown quite rapidly. The young woman A, standing apart, is seen at least once again; she has not moved at all. In this series there must finally be inserted certain new groups, which are not in the theater but in other salons of the hotel and at other times.

The theater images are thus succeeded by a series of views of the hotel and its inhabitants, in various places, at various times. These too are stationary shots, but their duration gradually increases. At the same time, the number of characters gradually diminishes and their position in the image becomes increasingly marginal. These scenes are composed as a function of the setting, so as to place some ornamental fragment (or else nothing at all) in the middle of the field of vision, gradually relegating the human beings to the sides, either in a more or less vague foreground (fragments of bodies, heads seen from behind, etc.) or in the background in the form of more organized groups.

The music has gradually faded, and here and there a word can be heard emerging from a chance phrase, such as: . . . *unbelievable . . . murder . . . actor . . . lying . . . had to . . . you're not . . . it was a long time ago . . . tomorrow . . .* etc.

Then, the music having grown quite calm, actually muted except for an occasional sudden burst of sound, long fragments of conversation can now be heard, such as:

. . . see any connection; there is no connection, my dear, absolutely no connection, and the fact that he, or she, might have said or done certain things that would suggest. . . .

Or else:

. . . and an impossible climate besides. No hope of setting foot outdoors for months on end, and suddenly, just when you least expect it. . . .

Or else:

Did you see him yourself?

No, but this friend of mine who told me about it. . . .
Oh, well then . . . told you. . . .

These fragments themselves being only partially comprehensible. Moreover the words grow slower as the rhythm of the series of shots abates.

29

The series of views of the hotel ends with a stationary shot possessing all the same characteristics, carried to their extreme. A slow scene. The image includes, at the far left, a blurred close-up of a man's head, cut by the edge of the image and not facing the camera. It is X, the hero of the film, but the spectator can hardly tell him from the other characters who have appeared in similar fashion in the preceding images. In the center of the screen in the middle distance is a clearly visible element of the setting: for instance a monumental mantelpiece with candelabras and a huge, elaborately framed mirror. Finally, to the right and in the background (preferably in another room, visible through a doorway), a man and a woman standing, talking in low voices. What they are saying is barely audible as a vague whispering.

X's head, in the foreground, then turns in this direction, but not abruptly; the direction of his gaze is not indicated explicitly: it must seem merely possible that X is looking at the couple. Neither the man nor the woman seems to pay any attention to X (who is, moreover, quite far away).

Their words are at first indistinct, virtually incomprehensible; then the volume rises slightly and we begin to understand the dialogue, particularly the man's remarks, for he speaks louder and louder.

MAN: *The others? Who are the others? Don't be so worried about what they are thinkng.*

WOMAN: *You know perfectly well....*

MAN: *I know you said you would listen to no one but me.*

WOMAN: *I am listening to you.*

30

During these remarks, the camera moves so as to center the image a little more on the couple, but without coming any closer, still keeping them almost in the background. During this movement, X's head leaves the field of vision.

From this moment on, the entire text is audible and distinct (though evidently situated at the rear of the set).

MAN: *Then listen to my complaints. I can't stand this role any longer. I can't stand this silence, these walls, these whispers you're imprisoning me in. . . .*

WOMAN: *Don't talk so loud, please don't.*

MAN: *These whisperings, worse than silence, that you're imprisoning me in. These days, worse than death, that we're living through here side by side, you and I, like coffins laid side by side underground in a frozen garden. . . .*

During these last words, the woman has looked away from the speaker; she stares anxiously in front of her (toward the camera) and glances to the right and left (but still forward), as if keeping watch on the surroundings.

WOMAN: *Be still!*

MAN: *A garden reassuringly arranged, with clipped bushes, and regular paths where we walk with measured steps, side by side, day after day, within arm's reach but without ever coming an inch closer to each other, without ever. . . .*

WOMAN: *Be still, be still!*

With these words, the woman begins walking forward, leaving her companion (who has remained stationary, like her, from the beginning of the scene). The man makes up his mind to follow her a few seconds later. They both advance side by side, about a foot and a half apart, toward the camera.

Silence. Only the sound of their approaching footsteps is heard, especially the woman's heels on the parquet, which is uncarpeted at this point.

When they have reached the foreground, the camera rotates so as to keep them within the frame while they continue walking without a word through the rooms, disappearing in another direction; the sound of their footsteps dies away.

The couple meets in passing—at a distance—two men (both very elegantly dressed, like everyone else seen since the beginning of the film and like everyone still to be seen) who are walking not in the opposite direction but at a different one (the trajectory of the two men makes, for instance, a right angle with that of the couple). The camera, which had been focused on the couple, then begins following the two men by a modification of its movement that is as natural as possible.

The two men are speaking in low voices. What they say is indistinguishable. The camera accompanies them at some distance, and perhaps quite vaguely. Other characters cross the screen at random; and fragments of bodies occasionally appear in close-up.

Snatches of phrases are heard, their sources unrevealed:

... *Really, that seems incredible. ...*
... *We've already met, long ago. ...*
... *I don't remember very well. It must have been in '28 or '29. ...*

At the same time, the music returns, imperceptibly; it is no longer the romantic strain of the beginning: it consists, on the contrary, of scattered notes or brief series of notes; it is uncertain, broken up, and somehow anxious.

As the two men pass in front of a third, who is examining a framed print hung on a wall (a print of a garden *à la française*, but scarcely discernible), the camera stops at this last character,

32

though he is seen from behind and without any particular charm, while the other two men leave the field of vision. The image includes (stationary shot), aside from the motionless character, a big mirror (the same one seen before above a mantlepiece) into whose field enters almost immediately the couple already seen the moment before, who stop while continuing their (inaudible) conversation quite a distance away.

Almost immediately: reverse angle, showing the man and woman without the intermediary of the mirror. They are in the same position and still quite far away, in the middle distance, a little lost in a very ornate, complicated setting (series of doorways). They are seen talking, but their dialogue cannot be heard. They are located toward the center of the screen, but somewhat to the left.

X's figure (head only, or a little more) appears in the foreground on the right side of the screen. X is looking toward the couple. The camera then changes position: it shifts slightly so as to center completely on the couple. During this movement, X is entirely eliminated from the field of vision.

The fragmentary music that had become a little more insistent at the end of the preceding shot has faded out as though from lack of conviction. Similarly, the chance phrases that were still heard (... *the summer of 1922 ... no one ever knew what happened afterward ... a very beautiful woman ... imagination ...*) have finally given way to a complete silence, in which the man's voice is heard, very low at first, but gradually recovering its customary volume.

MAN: ... *tolerate this silence, these walls, these whisperings worse than the silence you imprison me in these days we're living through here side by side, all alike one after the other, walking along these corridors with measured steps, within arm's reach but without ever coming an inch closer, without ever holding out to each other these fingers made to lock, these mouths made to ...*

WOMAN: *Be still, be still!*

And the shot abruptly changes.

New shot of the couple continuing their conversation. The characters are still farther away and are no longer in the center of the screen. And it is X's voice that continues instead of the man's. (But X remains invisible.)

X's VOICE: ... *these fingers made to clasp, these eyes made to see you, that must turn away from you—toward these walls covered with ornaments from another century, black woodwork, gilding, cut-glass mirrors, old portraits—stucco garlands with interlacing baroque ribbons—*trompe-l'oeil *capitals, false doors, false columns, painted perspectives.*

While this sentence is spoken offscreen with a certain deliberation and many pauses, several (not necessarily stationary) views are shown of the empty hotel: salons, corridors, doors, colonnades, etc., as though in search of characters now altogether missing. This sequence must develop without haste and continue, after X's voice has stopped, in complete silence for quite a long time.

Then abruptly (no dissolve) a salon full of people is shown (it might, for instance, be the salon that was shown empty at the end of the preceding sequence. The shot is taken from exactly the same angle).

In the foreground stands a group of three men and a woman talking with a polite animation. Evening dress. Farther on, other groups, sitting or standing; everything is quite stationary: without notable body movements.

The shot remains stationary during its whole first portion. The group does not occupy all or even the center of the field of vision.

The appearance of the salon full of people has been marked by the explosion of the noises of a party. But a sophisticated party, discreet noises, with a few audible words standing out against a vaguer hubbub. The impression of an explosion has been produced merely by a somewhat louder exclamation uttered by a character in the foreground, at the very moment the scene begins (at the same time as the image). This exclamation is the word:

Extraordinary!

After this initial exclamation, which stood out from the rest, there are vaguer murmurs which are mingled with those of the room. One of the men says something to the woman, but into her ear, and none of his words can be heard.

The third man, standing in the center (that is: neither the man who has uttered the exclamation nor the man who has spoken to the woman), then says:

A MAN: *Actually, it wasn't so extraordinary after all. He had started the whole thing himself, so that he knew all the possibilities in advance.*

Discreet laughter, accompanied by exclamations uttered half aloud, of the sort: *Oh well then. . . . If that's it. . . . That explains everything! . . . Still it's funny that. . .*

With the final exclamations and laughter, the camera begins sliding away and comes to a stop on another group of the same gathering (whose general arrangement remains static). It is again a couple, but younger than the previous one, smiling and at ease. This couple is farther away from the camera than the first group of four, but their conversation can be heard distinctly.

YOUNG MAN: *You haven't been here long?*

YOUNG WOMAN: *But I've already been here before, you know.*

YOUNG MAN: *Is it a place you like?*

YOUNG WOMAN: *Me? No, not particularly.* (Her words gradually lose their acoustic intensity and the end of the phrase can scarcely be heard.) *It's a matter of chance: we always come back here. My father had to. . .*

The camera draws closer to the young couple, at the same time as the sound of their voices fades (instead of growing louder). The young couple is then seen in a rather vague close-up, and the camera passes them, as if it had passed through them. The sound of their voices has disappeared completely. Having thus eliminated the couple, the camera comes to a stop with a stationary shot which reveals what was behind the couple.

It is, once again, the character standing apart, seen from behind, examining a print (of the garden) hanging on the wall. But he seems to be looking at the frame, not the picture. Almost immediately he turns his head away (he is now seen in profile) to look at something (invisible to the spectator, since it is located off-screen) which he continues staring at (a rather rapid shot).

During this scene, isolated phrases and half-comprehensible words have been heard without its being clear who has been speaking: . . . *trafficking in influence* . . . *it's always the same thing* . . . *people close their eyes* . . . *a shoe with a broken heel.* . .

Emerging somewhat more clearly from the confusion, a last phrase can be distinguished quite easily: . . . *and there's no way of escaping.* It's a woman's voice that has spoken; and immediately, as though echoing it, X's voice repeats, quite low but very near: . . . *and there's no way of escaping.* It is at this moment that the character turns his head to look at something offscreen, as if he were trying to find out who has just spoken. After a silence, another man's voice is heard, also offscreen, speaking the phrase *(Don't you know the story?)* immediately preceding the change of shot (see below).

Another stationary shot which may represent what the character above is looking at. It is a group of four people: A (the heroine), a man of about fifty (tall, gray-haired, with a good deal of "style," let us call him M) and two minor characters (a man already seen in the various groups and an elderly woman). M is standing—distant, smiling, motionless; the elderly woman is sitting in an armchair; the man already seen (an attractive, serious-looking man of forty) is sitting on the arm of another chair and telling a story. A is standing a little apart from the others; her eyes are fixed on the man talking; she is in exactly the same characteristic position as during her two first appearances.

The image shifts slightly as though to correct the composition of the group; the camera movement continues, giving the impression that it is A (standing slightly to one side) who should be in the center; but the movement does not stop when she is, and all the characters in the group are passed by, one after the other, including A. The movement of the camera continues regularly until the shot reaches a new group in conversation: two men sitting and one standing (already more or less familiar from the earlier salon scenes.) It is one of the two seated men who is speaking.

A man, then another (the first phrase is spoken offscreen at the end of the preceding shot of the first group): *Don't you know the story?* (New shot. The first speaker and his three listeners appear: A, M, and a man.) *It was all anyone talked about last year. Frank had convinced her he was a friend of her father's and had come to keep an eye on her. It was a funny kind of eye, of course. She realized it a little later: the night he tried to get into* (The camera has moved, and already neither the group nor the character talking can be seen, though his voice is still heard.) *her room, as though by accident and with some ridiculous excuse anyway: he claimed he wanted to tell her about the old pictures in her room. . . . There wasn't a single one there! But she didn't* (the camera movement having continued, what is now seen is the second group and the new speaker, whose voice seems to continue the first speaker's sentence.) *think of that at the time. The fact that he had a German passport didn't prove much. But his presence here has no connection, my dear, absolutely no con . . .*

The sentence is interrupted by a young woman's laughter, warm, deep and quite brief, entirely drowning out the man's voice.

The image is cut one or two seconds after the laughter begins. It is replaced by another shot of the first group which includes A; it is A who is laughing. The storyteller and the elderly lady are also smiling or laughing. Only M remains impassive (or with a very slight smile); he is still standing in the same position.

The image of this group immediately begins shifting in the same direction as before, making exactly the same trajectory as the first time and stopping in the same way at the group of three men standing nearby. But this group is no longer the same, al-

though composed in just the same way: two men sitting on either side of a small card table and a third man standing between the two, facing the camera. But now this standing man is M, and one of the two others (the one who wasn't talking previously) is X, the hero of the film. The only one who hasn't changed is the man who was talking about the German passport; but now he says nothing. (He is the first man in the group whom the camera discloses as it moves. Since he remains the same for both of his successive appearances, it seems at first that the rest of the group will also be the same as the first time.)

The beginning of the conversation between X and M takes place offscreen, as the image shifts toward their group.

M's VOICE: *No, not now.... I have another game to suggest instead: I know a game I always win....*

X's VOICE: *If you can't lose, it's not a game!*

M's VOICE: *I can lose.* (Short pause; M appears on the screen at this moment; it is he who is talking.)

M (continuing): *... But I always win.*

X: *Let's try.*

M (laying out the cards in front of X): *It takes two people to play. The cards are arranged like this. Seven. Five. Three. One. Each player picks up cards in turn, as many cards as he wants, on condition that he takes from only one row each time. The man who picks up the last card has lost.* (A brief pause, then pointing to the cards he has laid out:) *Would you like to start?*

M, standing quite rigidly, evidently in the same position as in the preceding shot, has laid out the cards in front of X according to the following diagram: They play quickly and in silence, without music. After a second's reflection X takes one card from the row of seven. M very quickly takes one card from the row of five. X reflects for three seconds and picks up the rest of the row of seven. M, still without pausing to think takes two cards from the row of five. X takes a card from this same row. M takes two cards from the row of three. X

```
0 0 0 0 0 0 0
  0 0 0 0 0
    0 0 0
      0
```

thinks for a few seconds, smiles as if he realizes he has lost, takes one of the cards that remain (row of five). M takes one of the others (row of three). A single card remains; since all the cards have been laid out face down, it is not seen what card this one is.

Yet the camera has moved closer to the table during the game and remains momentarily fixed on this remaining card, as if it had some meaning. The image is interrupted only at the moment of A's laughter (A is invisible), which is repeated just as before, after the last card has remained for X. This laughter lasts to the end of the shot and a little beyond.

Before this laughter is over, an image of A is shown, a close-up of her head and bust. She is not laughing at all, her face is frozen, expressionless, merely beautiful. Yet her laughter can still be heard, continuing for several seconds. Only A can be seen clearly, but there are also one or two distant groups shown from behind, partly cut off by the edges of the screen. After quite a long silence, X's voice is heard again (X is still invisible), still near and low, clear and neutral, without the shot being changed.

X's VOICE: *You are still the same. It is as if I had left you yesterday.*

With a gap of a few seconds after the end of the sentence, A turns her head to one side. It had been seen in full face and is now shown in three-quarters. No doubt she is looking at something the spectator cannot see. Then follows an offscreen conversation between a man and a young woman whose voices seem to be quite near.

MAN'S VOICE: *What's become of you in all this time?*

YOUNG WOMAN'S VOICE: *Nothing, as you see, since I'm still the same.*

MAN'S VOICE: *You haven't gotten married?*

During this dialogue A's face has remained motionless, her eyes still staring in the same direction.

Just after the last sentence, the shot changes and the new shot may be presumed to show what A is looking at (though this cannot be proved). We now see another corner of the same salon, with a group of two people standing in the center of the image: a man (perhaps someone already seen) and a young woman (the one previously seen in the young couple); but they are in the background, quite far away. They are talking, smiling, etc. They have not quite stopped walking, they take two steps forward. Their voices are heard as if they were very near, continuing the previous conversation.

YOUNG WOMAN: *Oh, no!*

MAN: *You're mistaken. It's a lot of fun.*

YOUNG WOMAN: *I like my freedom.*

New shot of the couple, this time quite close and stationary (in the same place as a moment before). The dialogue continues, light and playful.

MAN: *Here, for instance?*

YOUNG WOMAN: *Why not here?*

MAN: *It's a strange spot.*

YOUNG WOMAN: *You mean: to be free?*

MAN: *To be free, yes, that in particular.*

41

YOUNG WOMAN: *You're still as . . .*

The man and the young woman take a step or two toward the side of the screen and A appears behind them, a little farther away, motionless and staring straight at the camera. (Is it possible that she becomes gradually more distinct although remaining at a distance, while the characters standing to one side in the foreground grow blurred?)

The couple take several steps more and thus leave the screen during the last phrase spoken by the young woman. The latter's voice has stopped immediately. Then X's voice is heard again offscreen.

X's VOICE: *You're still as beautiful.*

The camera begins moving forward, getting closer to A, but at this moment other characters come between the camera and A, who disappears entirely.

Stationary shot of the corridors and salons; there are people here and there. A is still seen in the background to one side; but she passes and immediately leaves the screen.

Another shot of the same kind: a monumental staircase, for instance. There are still several characters, though less numerous than in the preceding image, and this time A is not there at all.

Three or four more stationary shots follow, showing characteristic views of the hotel, some of which may already have been used in the beginning of the film. There are fewer and fewer characters. The setting assumes a constantly increasing importance. These shots must follow each other rather fast.

During these shots, and without relation to what they represent, there is heard, without apparent reason, either when the shot changes or in the middle of a shot, a random number of irritating noises such as electric buzzers, sounds of automatic doors, telephone bells, etc., all of which should be unexpected and yet justifiable in terms of plausibility: they are all noises that can be readily heard in a hotel. Moreover they must be both extremely distinct and somehow muted, muffled by the carpets, etc. Lastly, they must be heard against a background of silence, of which they occupy only a very few moments.

This sequence ends with a view of the same kind, also stationary, which lasts a little longer. A single character is visible, in the distance. It is A, again in the characteristic pose she had assumed at her first appearance in the film.

The shot no longer includes any of the preceding noises. After a few seconds of absolute silence, X's voice is heard, still the same but even lower.

X's VOICE: *But you scarcely seem to remember.*

A turns her head rather quickly left and right, like someone trying to find out the source of the phrase just spoken.

Two or three stationary shots of salons and empty hallways which might represent for the spectator what A has just seen when she turned her head left and right.

There is no longer a single person on the screen; even the furniture is increasingly less apparent during this sequence.

(Thus, since the disappearance of the man and the young woman, the number of visible persons has steadily decreased: the scattered crowd giving way to several isolated guests and frozen servants, then A alone, then empty rooms; then doors, walls, columns, ornaments, etc., but without furniture.)

A very brief shot may be woven into this sequence, appearing as though by error: the garden *à la française*. (A quite characteristic bit of this garden with balustrade, statue, etc., without a single person in it.)

During these stationary shots music is heard, muted at first,

then more clearly, consisting of discontinuous notes (piano, percussion or classical instruments), with many gaps, silences of varying length (as in certain serial compositions). This music continues during the camera movements that follow, without further increasing in volume.

The camera moves closer to a decorative detail of the last image —a detail of extreme complexity in baroque or turn-of-the-century style and located well above eye level: a sconce for instance, or a sculptured frieze along the top of the wall, or the capital of a column, or a decorated ceiling. The photograph is taken from below, as if the detail were seen by an (invisible) character. But the camera moves nearer to examine the detail at close range (probably much more closely than would be possible for a man of normal height, without climbing up on a ladder) then turns around the chosen object in order to reveal its various elements, in the manner of documentary films on architecture. The music continuing a few minutes more, X's voice is heard, at first very low then gradually resuming its normal volume, while the music on the contrary gradually fades out. X speaks in the same beautiful neutral and exact voice, quite near, as it has already sounded on several occasions.

X's VOICE: *Yet you already know these baroque ornaments, these decorated lintels, these scrolls, this stucco hand holding a cluster of grapes.... The extended forefinger seems to be holding back a grape about to fall.*

(This text, offered as an example, happened to correspond to the actual setting used for this shot.) The description should be very anonymous, suggesting the "commentary" in an art film. Then the *you* reappears.

X's VOICE: *Behind the hand, you glimpse the foliage ... like the living leaves of a garden that is waiting for us.*

When X's voice refers to the leaves, this detail is not yet visible. Only when the description is over does the camera make the movement necessary (preferably a rotation) for the spectator to discover it.

In this movement, a man's hand, forefinger pointing toward the detail in question, appears in a lower corner of the screen. And

45

A's laughter is heard, quite brief but still the same: a warm, throaty laugh, though remaining quite polite.

The camera immediately moves back and down. X is seen, then A, to whom X is showing the detail in question (the hand is his, the voice too). They exchange two remarks with half-joking, half-serious expressions.

X: *Hadn't you ever noticed all this?*

A: *I never had such a good guide.*

The camera continues moving, and it is apparent that X and A are not alone; there is in particular a group of three persons quite near them, including M who, standing a little to one side, is watching X (but not ostentatiously: this must leave only a fugitive impression). One of the other characters present then says to A: *You know the saying: from the compass to the ship . . .*

X: (continuing the conversation with A): *There are lots of other things to see here, if you want to.*

Abrupt cut: although X and A are still close to each other, evidently at the same place on the screen as in the preceding shot, the scene is now entirely different: a dance in another salon; X and A are dancing and talking together in the middle of a crowd of other dancers, but not too thick a crowd, for the couples are not in each other's way.

A's first phrase sounded as though it belonged to the same conversation as in the preceding shot.

A: *I'd love to. Does this hotel contain so many secrets?*

Gradually the hubbub of the room and the dance music become noticeable.

X: *An enormous number.*

A: *What a mysterious look!*

The hubbub of the room and the dance music have become audible to normal hearing, but these people are not noisy, and the music is very gentle. X does not answer.

A (continuing): *Why are you staring at me like that?*

X does not answer immediately. After another silence he says, in a lower voice:

X: *You hardly seem to remember me.*

This is a stationary shot, and after a few exchanges, because of the movement of the couples, X and A have gradually shifted to the background and soon other dancers come between them and the camera, just when X has spoken his last phrase and as A looks at him with evident astonishment.

The shot lasts a few seconds more after they have completely disappeared.

It is followed by a more comprehensive view of the room and of the crowd of dancers—a view taken from as high up as possible. A slow, rhythmic but orderly animation is observable, suggesting Brownian movement. The dance is worldly and old-fashioned (preferably a waltz).

General hubbub of the dance floor, though without the slightest disorder. The music becomes louder, gradually growing quite insistent: a somewhat grandiloquent and stilted waltz, with many strings playing together.

Abruptly: after a climax of the music, cut short at its peak, a silent, motionless shot. Five or six men are standing in a row in a shooting gallery. They are no longer in evening clothes, but are scarcely less "dressed up," even so (smoking jackets, dark colors). They are facing the camera with their backs to the (invisible) targets. They are standing motionless and rigid, arms alongside their bodies with pistols in their right hands, barrels pointing

47

down; their eyes are staring into space like soldiers at attention. No one moves.

After a certain time (five seconds or even ten), the first man in the row turns around with a single movement, raises his arm and immediately fires, aiming only by guesswork. Immediately afterward, the second man executes the same maneuver. The third, etc. It might be supposed that each man has a signal in front of him: he turns around when the signal lights up. But the signals are not shown.

The pistol shots follow each other regularly. The sound of the explosions is very violent. Between the detonations (accompanied perhaps by the percussion of the bullet against the iron plate that must be behind the target), nothing can be heard.

The shot changes, now showing the row of targets. The first are already perforated. Those following are not, but a hole appears near the center of each one, in the same rhythm as before. On the screen, only six or seven targets can be seen, but the photograph should be taken in such a way as to indicate that their total number is perhaps higher.

The series of detonations (and percussions) continue regularly in this shot, perhaps every three seconds. There have been four detonations in the preceding shot. The shot ends precisely on a detonation.

New shot of the row of marksmen facing the camera, pistols held alongside their bodies. The targets are behind them, invisible to the spectator. This time as well, six men or perhaps slightly more are seen; but as before, the presence of others must be suggested, the screen showing only a section of the row that continues in each direction. (The first time, the row could extend in only one direction—that is, after the last man seen: there was, in fact, no marksman standing before the first one seen since no detonation was heard before the shot he fired.)

Although the photograph shows the men's bodies in precisely the same arrangement as the first time, these are not quite the same people: the first man of the row now visible was in the middle of the initial row; the others then follow in the same order; hence three marksmen already seen the first time are visible and three new marksmen who come after them. The first of these new marksmen is X.

After a moment's immobility, the same ritual is repeated: the marksmen turn around one after the other to fire and then remain facing the target (their backs, consequently, to the camera). Their gestures have the same precise and mechanical quality, but the rhythm is much quicker (perhaps accelerated in relation to the camera speed). The image is cut at the very moment when X turns around to fire.

This scene, before the pistol shots begin, is not absolutely silent, unlike the same scene shown previously. The preceding shot (in which the targets were shown) ended with an explosion. With the image that follows it (that is, the row of marksmen again), nothing can be heard at first; but after three or four seconds, a distinct ticking of a clock can be (gradually) heard.

As the ticking grows entirely audible, almost loud, the first detonation of the new series is heard (though no one has moved: there must be a marksman not shown on the screen), then the second (another invisible marksman, for all the visible characters have remained motionless); it is at this point that the first visible man turns around and fires and the third detonation-percussion is heard.

This sequence could be quite rapid throughout, or else, on the contrary, accelerate after a first interval which would be identical to that of the initial sequence. The image is cut at the moment X turns around; this last detonation is not heard.

There follow three brief motionless images which must succeed each other at the rhythm of the pistol shots of the preceding scene:

1) Close-up of one of the targets, with those on each side.

2) Close-up of X's face, frozen, calm, but tense.

3) A characteristic view of the hotel salons and corridors, with no one visible. It is exactly the same shot as the one in which A was seen alone, in the background, in the last series of salons, corridors and stairways (with the characters gradually disappearing). In all these shots of the hotel, there are never any windows; or, in any case, the landscape outside is never shown, nor even the windowpanes.

The shot remaining the same, A appears from the rear (emerging from the shadow of a complicated passageway: a series of doors, columns, etc.). She takes only a few steps forward and stops, looking toward the camera, in exactly the same pose as at the beginning of the image discussed in the paragraph above (the characteristic pose from the beginning of the film).

There are no further detonations nor any more ticking sounds. The two first shots are silent. There is only, at each cut, the sound of a door slamming, already heard among the irritating noises of the hotel. This is not a loud reverberation, but a simple click, distinct as that of a bolt in a lock. The third shot, which shows an empty room, then A coming in at the rear of the set, is at first silent too, without music. Then a pistol shot is heard, but remote and muffled. It is at this moment that A stops. Then there is complete silence again.

After about five seconds, X's voice is again heard offscreen, very close but rather low at first, then gradually assuming its usual intensity, while the camera begins moving closer to A.

X's VOICE: *The first time I saw you was in the gardens of Frederiks-bad. . . .*

Short silence, the voice continues, still quite near, but a little louder:

X's VOICE: *You were alone, standing a little apart from the others, against a stone balustrade on which your hand was resting, your arm half extended. You were facing a little to one side, toward the broad center path, and you hadn't seen me coming. Only the sound of my footsteps on the gravel finally attracted your attention, and you turned your head.*

A remains motionless, showing her full face, as the camera moves toward her, very slowly and steadily. A's features, which had expressed a certain tension at the sound of the distant pistol shot, have afterwards (immediately, gradually) become perfectly calm again. The camera movement ends with a close-up of her face, which is quite smooth (it seems merely beautiful, absent, "varnished"). This stationary image continues for a certain time while X's voice, offscreen, continues describing the garden and A's pose against the balustrade.

Then A's face moves slightly, her head bows a little and a smile appears on her mouth and in her eyes. She ends by smiling fully, with a kind of remote politeness, and says:

A: *I don't think I'm the person you mean. You must be making a mistake.*

At the same time, the camera moves back (making a rotation) and it is seen that A is not alone: X is standing beside her; other people are also near them, guests already seen before (those, for instance, who were with them in the groups, but not M). X then answers, and his words can now be followed on his lips as he continues talking, the image still representing the present dialogue (in a salon of the hotel) and not the garden scene described by X.

X: *Remember: quite near us there was a group of stone figures on a rather high base, a man and a woman in classical dress, whose frozen gestures seemed to represent some specific scene. You asked me who these characters were, I answered that I didn't know. You made several guesses, and I said that it could just as well be you and I.*

A, whose smile has returned, begins laughing aloud, a little polite, amused laugh that is soon over. X continues:

X: *Then you began laughing.*

The camera having continued the rotating movement begun above, A is now eliminated from the field of vision while X spoke this last phrase. The camera continues to shift slowly and steadily in the same direction, revealing other characters, while X adds, after a brief silence:

X: *I love—I already loved—to hear you laugh.*

Then X too is eliminated from the field of vision, but his voice, offscreen, continues speaking in the same calm and assured way, while still more people are seen (full face, in profile, from behind) nearby in the salon.

X's VOICE: *The others, around us, had come closer. Someone mentioned the statue's name; it consisted of mythological characters, gods or heroes of ancient Greece, or else, perhaps, an allegory, or something of the sort. You weren't listening any more, you seemed far away. Your eyes had once more grown serious and empty. You half turned away, to look down the broad central path again.*

The people now included on the screen form a more organized group, and X himself (whose voice is still heard) has appeared in this group, although the camera has continued to move in the same direction so that it is impossible for the image to have returned to its point of departure. X is shown from a three-quarters or rear view, and the spectator cannot tell with certainty whether he is talking or not. Moreover, his voice stops very quickly.

The camera stops moving when A is also back in the field of vision (the same remark applies as for X, concerning the rational justification of her presence at this point in the salon). A is in the position X's voice has just now described: standing, half turned away, staring into space, her eyes wide open, as if far away. X,

who hasn't moved since his reappearance, is watching her. (He was already watching her before she was visable to the spectator.)

The shot, which is stationary, lasts a few seconds. X and A are quite motionless; four or five people, belonging to the same group, have their backs more or less turned to the camera, concealing from the spectator something they are all looking at: probably a table. Other people, more or less scattered to the right and left (and in front?), belong to other groups that are not entirely visible.

A man's voice is heard which is not X's voice but that of someone else in the group, a voice rather muffled by distance and the position of the speaker (who is invisible and probably sitting at the table): *one, two, three, four, five, six, seven . . . one, two, three, four, five . . . one, two, three . . . one.* (The figures are clearly separated; the three dots represent a pause that is somewhat more emphatic.) The shot changes exactly after the last *one.*

Reverse angle showing the same central group seen from the other side. X is now facing the camera (he has not moved, and is staring a little to one side, not toward the center of the group); standing as are his neighbors, he is slightly behind the others. X is staring in the same direction as before, but A is no longer in this direction, she has disappeared from the group (hidden when the shot changed). As well as the people seen more or less from behind a moment before, two or three persons sitting around a small round table are now seen. On the table there is only an ash tray, an almost empty box of matches with its lid lying beside it and, finally, sixteen matches arranged according to the diagram shown above

53

in front of one of the seated characters (a man). M, standing opposite him, leans over the table a little. X is almost between the two. Ideally, the spectator would see at one glance the matches arranged on the table (clearly visible, shown from a little above, the two players, and X looking elsewhere, while all the other attentive faces, on the contrary, are focused on the game.

Then X, turning his head and lowering his eyes, looks toward the table like the others. At the same moment, his voice is heard, offscreen, ending his account, still in the same tone of objective narration:

X's VOICE: *And once again we were separated.*

Close-up of the table (polished mahogany, for instance, or some other very shiny substance) with the sixteen matches in rows and the players' hands, and perhaps other hands resting motionless nearby. A quick game is played, M's hands never hesitating, the other player making obvious hesitations: moving from one row to another before deciding, though rapidly nevertheless. The players either pick up the matches with their fingertips or push them across the table; M uses only the second method. The matches taken out of play form two little heaps on either side of the table.

The seated player takes the single match first. M takes one from the row of three. The seated player takes one from the row of seven. M takes one from the row of five. The seated player takes one from the row of three. M takes one from the row of seven. The seated player takes one from the row of five. M takes three from the row of seven. The seated player takes one from the row of five. M takes one from the row of three. The seated player takes one from the row of seven. M takes two from the row of five; one match remains in front of the seated player.

The entire game is played in complete silence, unless the faint noise of the matches can be heard sliding across the table, and other "realistic" noises of the same kind, giving the silence its peculiar quality. Upon the final play, an electric bell is heard, quite near and not too muffled by the distance and the carpets, lasting several seconds until the shot changes. It is cut short the instant the image changes.

Immediately: a new shot of the sixteen matches arranged in their proper order again. This image is absolutely the same as the one that begins the foregoing game.

But this time, after a few seconds' hesitation, the seated player's hand comes to rest, spread out, on the game, and with a circular gesture (not too quick a one) scrambles the arrangement of the matches. And he says in a more or less distinct fashion: *No, it's impossible.*

A few muffled exclamations can then be heard here and there among the observers, who partially disperse.

The shot changes to show the continuation of the same scene from a little farther away, revealing not only the table but the bodies of the players and onlookers as well. The end of the game provokes various movements among the audience. The seated player stands up and walks away; others leave too; the group is diminished and scatters. During this time X, who is now standing next to the table, has stretched out his hand toward the scattered matches and has slowly, carefully replaced them in their initial order. He leans over the table for a minute and considers it attentively. M, on the contrary, has straightened up and stepped back slightly; he looks at X, his arms folded or else in a similar position; he is silent, frozen.

This new shot is at first accompanied by the same various

noises: an armchair being moved, a voice saying: *Come for a walk around* ... Another voice, of which all that can be heard are the words: ... *Not yet arrived* ...

Then a bell rings, exactly like the one heard before: close and slightly muffled; it lasts three or four seconds. And then a complete silence follows while X finishes arranging the matches and remains staring at them in their proper order. No sound of conversation or movement can be heard now. It is at this moment that X says, looking up:

X: *And what if you were to play first?*

M immediately unfolds his arms, grimaces slightly and gestures to indicate his polite acquiescence, and with the same movement bends over to pick up a match; he will subsequently play the entire game with the same rapidity. X, on the contrary, plays slowly, but without appearing to hesitate; somehow a little absently, rather, although he seems to be concentrating his attention on the game.

M has first taken the single match, X takes one match from the row of three, M takes one from the row of five, X takes another from the row of three, M takes two from the row of seven, X takes the last from the row of three, M takes another from the row of seven, X takes one from the row of seven, M takes one from the row of five, X takes one from the row of seven, M takes one from the row of five, X takes one from the row of seven, M takes the last two matches from the row of five. There remains one match for X: the last in the row of seven.

At the moment when X has picked up his first match, his voice, offscreen, has continued, still the same:

X's VOICE: *And once again I walked on, alone, down these same*

corridors, through these same empty rooms, I passed these same colonnades, these same windowless galleries, I crossed these same thresholds, making my way as though by chance among the labyrinth of similar itineraries.

The last plays of the game take place in silence; X's voice having stopped, nothing else can be heard.

Sequence of moving shots showing stationary characters. Groups of people throughout the hotel in frozen attitudes, though without any supernatural quality: they are simply not moving; yet this does not keep them from occasionally having rather forced attitudes, a somewhat suspect immobility, but only slightly so: a somewhat unstable equilibrium, an incipient gesture, a position of relaxation but an uncomfortable one, etc. The camera moves around them, turns, comes back to its starting place, as though around figures in a waxworks museum. It is perhaps only the camera movements that give a strange quality to the characters' motionlessness.

The first group examined is the one from the preceding shot: the players and the table. M has straightened up and folded his arms again. X has one arm half extended toward the last match on the table. One or two curious onlookers remain, but their eyes are elsewhere. The camera shows them in detail, while X's voice offscreen continues. (X already no longer in the field of vision at this moment. The silence had lasted a certain time, previously, while X and M were seen.)

X's VOICE: *And once again everything was deserted in this huge hotel, everything was empty.*

Rather emphatic silence which lasts until the end of this group and well into the following.

Then there are other groups, through salons, halls, galleries and lobbies. People sitting at a table in front of full glasses. Relaxed, yet constrained gestures. Perhaps they are only a little bored. Instead of looking at the glasses and toward the center of the circle, many are staring beyond it, but not all in the same direction. The camera moves slowly around them; yet the shot must be rapid enough so that the characters' immobility does not seem too unlikely.

57

Similarly: people standing in a doorway, people at a bar, people frozen in the middle of a hand of bridge (thinking over a difficult play), etc. All these shots have the same characteristics that they have had from the beginning of the film: heavily decorated setting, evening dress, formal manners, dark but distinct and gleaming images. There are also servants frozen at attention, etc.

After a pause, X's voice has continued, accompanying the images as if it were commenting on them. Yet there are only a few points in common, and always a certain discrepancy between the visible elements and the spoken enumeration: chairs occupied, glasses full, keys hung on the reception desk rack, a letter the porter has just handed a young woman, etc.

X's VOICE: *Empty salons. Corridors. Salons. Doors. Doors. Salons. Empty chairs, deep armchairs, thick carpets. Heavy hangings. Stairs, steps. Steps, one after the other. Glass objects, objects still intact, empty glasses. A glass that falls, three, two, one, zero. Glass partition, letters, a letter lost. Keys hanging from their rings, in their assigned place, lined up in successive rows, numbered door keys. 309, 307, 305, 303, chandeliers. Chandeliers. Beads. Unsilvered mirrors. Mirrors. Empty corridors as far as the eye can see . . .*

Then the voice stops until the camera abandons the group it was showing, moving on to the next: three men standing in an open doorway (a rather monumental door, one of the three is leaning against the jamb). The voice begins again with the first images of this new group, as if it had waited in order to announce it just as it reached the screen.

X's VOICE: *And the garden, like everything else, was empty.*

The end of this group, as well as the next, includes no further words. There is complete silence at first, then the music consisting of scattered notes already heard earlier begins again: a serial-type composition played on various instruments (piano, percussion, woodwinds, etc.). For the uninitiated, it gives more an impression of "disorganization" than of "cacophony"; it must be both disquieting and discreet.

The last group of the sequence is standing in a setting already seen during the long initial traveling shot (after the credits): one

58

of the lateral corridors or adjacent halls, glimpsed in passing during the movement down the huge gallery. The camera having circled, as for the preceding groups (but quite rapidly), the frozen characters, returns quite naturally to the gallery seen at the beginning of the film and starts following it; like the first time, it is absolutely empty. The sign for the stage performance is still where it was, announcing, like the first time: *"Tonight only . . ."*

But this time, the movement does not end at the theater. Having taken another route, which seems scarcely different, at the end of the gallery, the camera reaches a room of ordinary size with many empty seats, chairs and armchairs grouped in twos, threes, fives, with or without tables between them. All these seats are unoccupied, the room is empty . . . or almost: a woman is sitting in an armchair, in the middle of a circle of chairs (that is, as if she were carrying on a conversation with people, but the other seats are empty). This woman is A. She is reading a small hard-cover book. The camera slowly approaches her from in front.

The music gradually fades, and X's voice is heard again off-screen, rather low at the start but still calm, assured, without excessive warmth.

X's VOICE: *It was last year.*

A silence. Then, as A continues reading without moving, X's voice continues, a little louder but in the same tone.

X's VOICE: *Have I changed so much then? —Or are you pretending not to recognize me?*

A looks up from her book and holds it half-closed on her lap. She is staring at the floor in front of her, without moving, her expression remote. The camera has come still closer, then stops.

X's VOICE: *A year already—or perhaps more. —You, at least, haven't changed. —You still have the same remote eyes, the same smile, the same sudden laugh, the same way of extending your arm as if to push something away, a child, a branch, and the same way of slowly raising your hand toward the hollow of your shoulder . . . and you are wearing the same perfume, too.*

At these last words, A raises her eyes toward the camera, which is at the eye level of a man standing up.

Immediately, a shot representing the garden. Very bright light, contrasting with the rather dim lighting of all the views which have appeared on the screen up to this point. Brilliant sunshine, clear shadows that are not too long. The image represents a part of a garden *à la française* with the same characteristics as shown in the prints: a regular garden virtually without vegetation (only some flat, rectangular lawns, bushes clipped in perfectly geometric shapes, broad gravel paths, stone stairways, terraces with stone balustrades) and here and there huge statues on rather high, square pedestals; kings and queens in ancient costume, mythological characters, ceremonial postures, frozen gestures, poses that seem to have a precise though unintelligible meaning; there are also pedestals without statues, with the name of a subject engraved on them.

The entire landscape is empty: without a single living being. A long, slow lateral movement of the camera, showing perspectives of paths, of cones arranged in rows, of exactly clipped hedges, etc.

X's VOICE: *Remember. It was in the gardens of Frederiksbad. . . .*

The camera stops on a solitary character, a woman standing, leaning against a stone balustrade. It is A, dressed in the same gown as in the shot where she is reading. The setting is a great deal like that of the theater scene shown at the beginning of the film.

X's VOICE: *You were alone, apart. You were leaning at a slight angle against a stone balustrade on which your hand was resting, your arm half extended. . . .*

61

The voice stops. A is not in the position indicated by the text being spoken: she is standing, as a matter of fact, quite close to the balustrade, perfectly vertical in relation to it (that is, staring straight ahead over the rail, perpendicular to the latter), and seen from behind in a three-quarters view in relation to the camera. She then corrects her position: she moves a little away from the balustrade, turns slightly to one side, extends one arm to rest her hand on the stone (whereas she had had both arms alongside her body) and stares toward the central path; she is then seen exactly from behind in relation to the camera. Near her stands the statue previously described by X. The ground between A and the camera is covered with gravel. A having corrected her position, X's voice continues immediately, as if it had waited only for this.

X's VOICE: *You are staring down the central path.*

After a brief silence (scarcely noticeable: one or two seconds) a sound is heard, coming closer: it is the characteristic and soon perfectly distinct sound of a man's footsteps on the gravel. Having reached the acoustic foreground, it suddenly stops.

At this sound, A has slowly, gracefully turned around to face the camera, but she retains a distant, absent expression, as if she saw no one. Moreover, X is not seen on the screen, only his voice is heard.

X's VOICE: *I walked forward toward you.* (A brief silence.) *But I stopped at a certain distance, and I looked at you. —You were turned toward me, now. Yet you didn't seem to see me. —I was*

*watching you. You made no sign. I told you that you looked
alive.*

After the word *alive,* but with a few seconds' delay, a smile
gradually appears on A's face, yet an absent smile that seems meant
for no one.

And while X's voice continues, the camera begins to turn toward the statue, which becomes the center of the image, while A,
on the contrary, disappears from the field of vision, while continuing to smile, motionless and frozen.

X's voice: *In answer, you merely smiled.*

Still focusing on the statues, the camera does not remain motionless. It begins turning around it, at the distance and the height
of a man's eye (that is, the statues are seen from below).

Then a sequence of stationary shots show more unexpected
aspects of the stone group, these photographs being taken by
imaginary observers placed anywhere: even high in the air (angles
impossible for mere strollers).

When X gives detailed explanations as to the significance of the
statues' gestures, the camera shows points of view illustrating his
motions. During X's entire account, neither X nor A is ever seen,
but only the statues, until A's laugh.

X's voice: *To say something, I talked about the statue. I told you
that the man wanted to keep the young woman from venturing
any farther: he had noticed something—no doubt a danger—
and he stopped his companion with a gesture of his hand. You*

answered that it was actually the woman who seemed to have seen something—but something marvelous—in front of them, which she was pointing to.

But this was not incompatible: the man and the woman have left their country, journeying on for days. They have just reached the top of a steep cliff. He is holding back his companion so that she doesn't go near the edge, while she points to the sea, at their feet, stretching to the horizon.

Then you asked me the names of the characters. I answered that it didn't matter. —You didn't agree with me, and you began giving them names, more or less at random, I think. . . . Pyrrhus and Andromache, Helen and Agammemnon . . . Then I said that it could just as well be you and I. . . . (A silence.) Or anyone.

At these last words, A's laughter is heard, as before, but a little more sustained, gayer.

Toward the middle of this laugh, the shot changes, reversing: A is seen again, her laugh almost over. She is now with X, who stands beside her in the image. He is no longer in evening dress; he still, however, looks extremely "dressed up," with a slightly old-fashioned smartness (for example, a carefully fitted suit coat over a fancy vest?). And A is no longer wearing the same gown (she is now wearing, for instance, a dress with a long full skirt and stiff petticoat, recalling the old "new look," about eight inches from the floor). They are in front of the stone balustrade, near the statue.

Their conversation continues, but directly presented, acted, instead of being reported indirectly by X's voice. A's attitude is almost the same as in the hotel scenes: smiling, agreeable, but a trifle ironic and mundane. X is noticeably different: less neutral, more urgent, livelier, less severe.

X: *Don't give them any name . . . They could have had so many other adventures. . . .*

A (pointing to a dog represented beside the people in the group of statues): *You're forgetting the dog. Why do they have a dog with them?*

X: *The dog isn't with them. He just happened to be passing.*

A: *But you can see that he's snuggling up to his mistress.*

X: *She's not his mistress. He's snuggling up to her because the pedestal is too narrow. Look at them over there* (he points to another statue located outside the field of vision), *they're the same ones and they don't have any dog with them. They are facing each other now. She's holding out her hand toward her friend's lips. But from closer range you'll see that she's looking somewhere else. . . . Are you coming?*

A: *No, I don't want to. . . . It's too far. . . .*

X: *Follow me, please.*

At the same time, X holds out his hand toward A, inviting her to follow him. But she, on the contrary, steps back a little, shaking her head.

In close-up: A shaking her head. Her face serious, faintly alarmed. Nothing of the setting can be discerned around this face.

X's voice is heard offscreen, repeating exactly, as though echoing A's (but a trifle more neutrally and distinctly lower):

X's VOICE: *Please.*

Almost immediately, the camera begins moving back very slowly. And the setting reappears around A. It is no longer the garden, but once again the hotel salon, the one where A was sitting alone, reading a book. But now X is also in the picture. And they are not in the same part of this salon. They are both standing. X is in evening dress as usual. A, on the contrary, has kept the same gown she was wearing in the garden scene, the same make-up, etc. Yet she is holding in her hand the book she was reading. There are not so many empty chairs around them—only a few. And also a few people here and there, sitting or standing. X is seen almost from behind in relation to the camera, A, on the contrary, almost in full face.

As the camera moves back, A, while still making—slower—signs of denial, says:

A: *I tell you it's impossible. I've never even been to Frederiksbad.*

X: *Well, then it was somewhere else, maybe* (X can appear on the screen only after having already spoken this first phrase), *at Karlstadt, at Marienbad, or at Baden-Salsa—or even here, in this salon. You have followed me here so that I can show you this picture.*

In saying *that I can show you this picture,* X turns toward the camera. A, without noticeably moving her body, also looks in this direction. She is standing a little behind him, to one side, at a certain distance (one to two yards).

The moment X's face is seen straight on, the shot changes: a reverse angle showing the salon wall, on which hangs a large drawing, elaborately framed and exactly copied from the real setting that will be used later on: it shows, in the background, the whole front of the hotel and, in the foreground, a statue which is the one A was standing next to in the garden. X's voice is heard offscreen, describing the statue, although it is the hotel itself that strikes the attention in the drawing.

X's VOICE: *Look, you can distinguish the man's movement and the gesture the young woman is making with her arm. But you would have to be on the other side to see . . .*

The shot showing the drawing alone is very brief. Almost immediately it is succeeded by a new shot of the same scene taken from a little farther away. The drawing is smaller and partially concealed; now X and A are seen in the shot, located exactly in relation to each other as they were after turning around toward the wall. They are thus seen from behind, or almost.

X's explanations continue in this new shot, but something is gradually happening on the sound track which makes it strange, then obviously distorted, and the words become hard to follow. (Could this be two identical sound tracks run off at gradually differing speeds? Or else two sound tracks starting at different speeds, one of which being at first very faint and only gradually disturbing the principal track?)

When X's words have become absolutely incomprehensible, A turns around toward the camera. She is smiling, but her smile is no longer the same. It is both more familiar and somehow a little strained. It is evidently meant for someone this time. As when she had looked at the picture hanging on the wall, A has not moved her body more than is absolutely necessary: head and bust in particular.

Seeing that she is no longer listening to him (sensing this, rather), X stops talking and turns around too, but all in one movement, his entire body executing the rotation so that he is facing the camera.

Immediately the shot changes: a reverse angle showing X exactly from behind and A half-turning. They are then in exactly the respective positions they occupied before turning toward the print, but the postures are not quite the same: instead of looking at one another, they are both looking at a third person who has appeared between them, a little behind A (who is already a little behind X, who is closest to the camera). This person is M. He is in the familiar posture that has already been shown once or twice: arms folded, or something of this kind. M immediately begins talking, in a polite, faintly ironic voice that can still pass for that of someone eager to do a favor.

M: *Excuse me, sir. I think I can supply you with some more precise information: this statue represents Charles III and his wife, but it does not date from that period, of course. The scene is that of the oath before the Diet, at the moment of the trial for treason. The classical costumes are purely conventional. . . .*

The shot has changed in the middle of this speech, which continues offscreen during the new shot. The statue M is talking about is visible in the latter, but it does not occupy the center of the image, devoted to A herself, alone again in the garden, leaning

against the stone balustrade. A takes precisely the position the camera had discovered her in here the first time. After a few seconds, she half turns from the balustrade to look toward the statue (this movement is contrary to the one she made in order to look down the central path). The shot is cut very quickly; at the same time, M's voice stops in the middle of a sentence.

The first seconds of the new shot are absolutely silent. But gradually the serial music already heard several times begins. It is merely more consistent here, it produces less an effect of scattered notes. Gradually it achieves an intensity of considerable importance; it might well drown out the words spoken in the following shots, during which it continues.

First X is seen (full face) walking slowly but without hesitation in the long gallery. But his movement is in the opposite direction to the camera's at the beginning of the film. He is looking straight ahead, neither toward the pictures nor toward the windows, both of which, moreover, are scarcely visible because of the effect of the perspective.

Then a short stationary shot of a deserted corridor or lobby.

Then a sequence of stationary, brief shots, showing various corners of salons, generally, though not necessarily night views, with groups either talking, playing cards, or doing nothing at all. The conversations (which are not audible) are obviously not very animated. Can a gambling room, on the roulette table order, also be shown? In certain of these images A is present, often at the same time as M; on the contrary, X is never seen. A must always look vague, even turning away from the group where she appears, staring elsewhere, smiling absently sometimes, but always beautiful, graceful. When A is in the image the shot lasts a trifle longer. One or two shots of empty corridors may also be introduced in the sequence, as well as certain shots already seen during conversations in the salons or at the end of the play (exact repetition of the images, but without the words).

Unless the director has other ideas for enlivening this rather somber sequence, it might be embellished (made both less tiresome and more unendurable) by a violent noise at each change of shot: the detonation of the pistol accompanied by the sound of the bullet's percussion against the iron sheet. The first detonation

70

would take place at the end of the scene where X is walking along the gallery, then again at the end of each shot, the intervals being the same. But each time that A appears on the screen, the interval increases slightly, and the sound of the detonation grows more muffled. The next change re-establishes the original interval, but keeps the sound muffled. Hence the sound becomes gradually fainter. At the end it is scarcely more than a distant detonation that almost dissolves into the music that has continued steadily during this whole time.

The last image of the sequence shows A alone. She is near a table or some other low piece of furniture on which is placed a vase with a bouquet of flowers. One of the flowers (rose, peony, etc.) has shed its petals on the table. A picks up the fallen petals, one by one, slowly, and arranges them in front of her according to the diagram of the match game: a row of seven, a row of five, a row of three, a single petal. A must seem remote, and not sentimental.

The music, which had remained quite loud during the entire preceding sequence, gradually fades while A arranges the petals, which lasts a long time (in comparison with the rapidity of the preceding shots).

After a moment's silence, while A contemplates the petals arranged in front of her, the sound of a man's footsteps approaching across gravel is distinctly heard, as in the garden scene. Coming quite close, they suddenly stop. Complete silence again.

At the sound of the footsteps across the gravel (there is no gravel in the salon, of course!), A slowly raises her face and remains in this position for several seconds, motionless and mute, looking fixedly at the camera (that is, staring slightly to one side of the lens, according to the traditional procedure).

Reverse angle: X's face, also motionless and frozen, staring fixedly at the camera. After a few seconds, he says, in a voice both neutral and assured, not at all questioning:

X: *You were waiting for me.*

Again A's face; she answers without smiling, imperceptibly hostile for all her politeness:

71

A: *No . . . Why should I be waiting for you?*

X's face; he answers, in the same assured voice:

X: *I have waited for you, myself, a long time.*

A's face; she answers, this time with a slight smile, empty and polite, but pretty. Her brief phrase spoken, the smile freezes and disappears.

A: *In your dreams?*

X's face; he continues to stare directly at the camera, imperturbable, calm and severe. Whereas the four preceding shots, evidently of the same length, constituted a normal (and rapid) exchange in which the character speaking was seen each time, this shot continues during the following lines: X, having spoken his phrase, remains on the screen without speaking, while A is heard answering; then X speaks again; then he too stops talking again while A's answer is heard.

X: *And are you trying to escape again?*

He speaks more slowly than A, more regularly.

A's VOICE: *But what do you mean? I don't understand a thing you say.* (Hearing this, X smiles very quickly.)

X: *If they were dreams, why would you be afraid?*

A's VOICE: *Well, go on and tell me the rest of our story!* (Ironic tone; X remains impassive.)

At the last word, the shot changes and A's face is seen again, with a faint, ironic smile, while X's answer is heard. This shot and the three that follow function in the same way: the face of one of the interlocutors is seen and the voice of the other heard, alternately. The faces are in close-up, looking just as they did during the normal conversation.

On the shot of A's face, X's voice waits several seconds before continuing, still in the same tone of objective narrative:

X's VOICE: *We saw each other again during the afternoon of the same day.*

X's face, silent, listening to A's answer. X's features retain a kind of impassive tension, which contrasts with A's smiling voice:

A's VOICE: *By accident, of course?*

A's face smiling. X's tone is a little more remote.

X's VOICE: *I don't know.*

X's face, still the same; however A's phrase provokes a change, a kind of faint smile, whereas A's tone has again become more hostile:

A's VOICE: *And where was it, this time?*

View of the garden: a long path in perspective, between two narrow lawns (or rows of low, clipped bushes, or something of this kind that marks the vanishing point). In the background, the façade of the hotel, as it appears on the drawing decorating the wall in one of the salons.

In the distance, coming from the hotel, or from a side path concealed by the bushes, a woman enters the field of vision, at first a tiny silhouette, then coming closer to the camera, walking directly toward it from the opposite end of the path. It is A, in the same gown as during the scene near the statue. She is walking a little too fast for someone merely strolling; she glances alternately right and left several times during her straight course, as if she were looking for someone. After a moment, she turns into a perpendicular path, but only takes a few steps in this direction and returns to her initial route, which she continues to follow, sometimes looking down at her feet, sometimes toward the camera, sometimes to the right or left again (generally she looks at her feet, and only occasionally glances up or to one side). Around her, no one else can be seen. She seems a little lost in the empty garden. Soon it is apparent that she is walking in her stocking feet, and holding her delicate shoes in one hand.

The camera, after a certain length of time, begins moving back, so as to keep A from reaching the foreground, and in its movement reveals the rest of the long path. A tries again to escape, turning at right angles in the opposite direction to her first turn, but again she gives up and returns to her original course.

Although this entire walk is a little too rapid for a stroll, it must not give any impression of running, or of excitement; the turns themselves must be plausible: executed naturally enough, or even justified by some element of the setting. (Perhaps, on the contrary, it will be necessary to cut the images where the actress retraces her steps, continuing only when she is back on the path and again advancing toward the camera; which would avoid having to justify the about-face.) A's face should be calm and empty, only a trifle tense at moments, not at all upset.

The beginning of the scene is completely silent, with neither music nor speech. Then X's voice offscreen, in a somehow distant tone, though actually quite close, repeats A's question.

X's voice: *Where was it. . . . That doesn't matter.*

Then comes a long, complete silence, while A continues advancing down the path.

74

Then the voice continues offscreen:

X's VOICE: *You were in the middle of a group of friends—casual friends—people I scarcely knew—and perhaps you knew them no better than I.* (A pause.) *They were talking, in a joking, informal way, about some affair of the moment about which I knew nothing.* (A pause.) *You yourself were better informed about it than I, no doubt—I was watching you.* (A pause. At this moment, A raises her eyes, looking right and left, without stopping in her advance toward the camera.) *You were taking part in the conversation with an animation that seemed false to me. It was as if no one knew who you were, among all those people, as if I was the only one to know. And you didn't know it either.* (A pause.) *But you still avoided meeting my eyes. Apparently you were doing it on purpose—systematically.*

A has just turned into a side path. X's voice stops, only resuming when A is again on the central path she has been following since the beginning.

X's VOICE: *I was waiting. I had time.* (A pause.) *I have always believed I had time.* (Another pause, distinctly longer than the others.)

The voice resumes:

X's VOICE: *Your eyes, moving from one face to the next, passed over me as if I didn't exist.* (A pause, rather a short one. Then,

in a more animated tone:) *To force you to see me, finally, I said something myself, suddenly taking part in the conversation by making a rather outrageous remark that would suddenly attract attention to me. —I don't remember what it was any more.*

At this last phrase, A has stood perfectly still, raising her eyes toward the camera. The camera has stopped moving back, though A is still continuing to walk forward, so that the young woman has now reached the foreground, as if there were no longer any space between her and the lens. The shot immediately changes.

Reverse angle, showing a group of persons in the same garden. A is seen from behind, in exactly the same place and the same position as in the preceding shot, but she has her shoes on. She is closest to the camera; the others are located at varying distances, forming a rather loose group, distributed between her and a stone balustrade (as if this balustrade stood at the end of the long path). The characters are precisely the ones who were watching the game with the sixteen matches. M is part of the group, as is X.

Some of the characters are standing, others are leaning against the balustrade or even half-sitting on it. There could be a statue (or a pedestal) in the immediate vicinity. Everyone is motionless. X is looking at A; M is looking at X; the others are looking at each other.

Then everyone, more or less together, turns toward X, as though toward someone who has just spoken. A is the last to make this movement. X gradually begins to smile: a somewhat distant, rather ambiguous half-smile.

X's voice resumes, offscreen, and the heads turn one after the other toward A (whose face is still not seen, since her back is to the camera). X's smile fades, or freezes. M is the only one to remain turned toward X.

X's VOICE: *You're the one who answered me, in the sudden silence, with an ironic phrase about the implausibility of my remark.* (A pause.) *The others said nothing. —Again I had the impression that no one understood your words, perhaps even that I was the only one who heard them.*

On the *perhaps even* the image has changed: close-up of A's face, serious, rather tense.

Then follows a sequence of close-ups of the faces of the group. All the faces are frozen, like those of people listening to something, straining to hear noises, somewhat tense but without anxiety. The photographs are taken full face or in profile. The poses are natural, but often the heads are somewhat bent; the only heads to be perfectly upright are those of X (still full face) and M (in profile).

After the close-up of A, X is seen first, then a face, then another, then X again (exact repetition of the same shot), then faces of other minor characters, then M, then X again.

The sound of a large orchestra tuning up is heard, gradually increasing in volume. At first there are several isolated sounds, then a whole group of various and discordant sounds, against

which louder notes stand out: a few chords, here and there, of the waltz heard during the dance scene.

During this sequence the light has gradually faded. At the same time the background of the garden has become less distinct. The last image of X is against a completely black background.

Continuing this sequence, at the same rather rapid rhythm, another close-up of the same kind of frozen face is seen, but this is no longer one of the characters from the garden scene, and the lighter background would allow a practiced eye to identify a salon of the hotel. Then one or two more similar shots follow, still at the same rhythm. Then again X's face, and in the background, the ballroom already seen earlier. As during his previous appearances, X is looking fixedly at the camera, without a smile, but also as though without any specific intention.

The sounds of the orchestra tuning up have been suddenly interrupted and followed by absolute silence (have the conductor's baton taps been heard, struck against the music stand to call for silence?).

Then X's voice continues offscreen.

X's VOICE: *To break the silence, someone spoke of the entertainments arranged for the evening or for the next day—or for the following days. —I don't remember any more what we said afterward.*

X's words should end during the close-ups of the faces from the ballroom. Then there is total silence, on a shot of a last dancer's face, then on X's face which has returned to the screen, quite motionless, like all the preceding faces.

At the end of the last shot, with sudden violence, the large orchestra is heard playing a waltz; very heavily scored music (many strings played together), pompous and a little formal, and at the same time passionate, although slow.

Another close-up: X and A dancing a very slow, dignified waltz (partners quite far from each other, postures without languor, etc.). X should appear on the screen in approximately the same place as in the preceding shot, and still in full face. A is in profile, or seen in a three-quarters view from behind. She is not looking at X. This is probably not a stationary shot: the camera

moves, but very slightly, in order to follow the couple's slow gyrations. At this moment nothing more can be seen than the two heads and the upper part of the two bodies.

The waltz music continues through all the following shots, without interruption. It is the same music of which several measures have already been heard in the first dance scene. It remains slow and noble, very heavily orchestrated, almost deafening at moments.

New shot of the dance: the same couple seen from below. And other couples around them, but not an excessive number. The transition from the preceding shot to the latter was a slow dissolve, one image gradually fading and the next gradually appearing.

X and A are still dancing the same distance from each other. X is looking at A, but not insistently. A is looking elsewhere. They do not talk to each other.

Dissolve, identical to the preceding one. The new image shows people in one of the salons; slow, measured gestures; conversations inaudible (no sound track) on account of the music. Preferably one of the shots already used in one of the rapid sequences. Neither A nor X nor M is seen. This shot lasts a little longer than the first time.

Dissolve, identical to the preceding ones. The new image represents a poker table. Five or six players, including M and X. The cards have already been dealt and the players no longer need to look at their hands. The cards are lying on the table, face down naturally, or held in stacks. The players also have piles of chips beside them. In the center, another pile of chips represents the bets already made.

All the players are silent. One after the other, the players around the table add chips to the central pile, according to the rules. They never consult their cards for this, even if they hesitate a little before betting. They merely watch each others' faces discreetly, without insisting unnecessarily. Virtually no one speaks. They are tense but as though without passion, efficient and absent at the same time.

M having bet a large number of chips, the other players hesitate a little longer, and some withdraw; the others meet the bet; X bets a little more; the last adversaries withdraw. (A player who withdraws places his cards, without showing them, in the center of the table, along with the cards left over from the deal.) Only M and X remain in the game: the others watch them, or look elsewhere. X and M raise the bets two or three times more, then M having suddenly bet a larger number of chips, X reflects for a second, looks at M and gives up, throwing his cards in with the others. M smiles, gathers up all the chips in the center of the table and places his cards with the rest. Neither he nor X have showed their hands. M picks up all the cards and begins shuffling them.

During the game, the waltz music has faded, and X's voice is heard again offscreen, accompanying the whole game.

X's VOICE: *You didn't much like walking in the park, because the gravel was uncomfortable to walk on in your street shoes.... One day, but it was most likely later on, you even broke one of your high heels. You had to take my arm for support, while you removed your shoe. The heel was almost off, held only by a thin strip of leather. You stood there staring at it for a minute, the tip of your bare foot on the ground, a little ahead of the other one, in the pose of a dancer at school.... I suggested going to find you another pair. You didn't accept my offer. Then I said that I could also carry you back in my arms. You merely laughed, without answering, as if it was...* (A pause.) *You must have carried your shoes back to the hotel that day, walking barefoot across the gravel.*

Dissolve, identical to the preceding ones ... ending back in the ballroom. X and A are still dancing the same waltz (in the interval A may have changed dresses; but this is not indispensable). The dance is coming to an end: after a few measures the couples stop, as does the music, which had recovered all its intensity; the end of a classic, rather grandiloquent waltz.

The men bow politely in front of their partners, at a certain distance. X and A who are still in the foreground, executing this figure. Then the dancers disperse. X leads A, still very formally, toward a bar close by. The orchestra has stopped. General hubbub of the room, though polite and discreet. No words can be discerned, except this phrase spoken by X: *Would you like something to drink?*

A doesn't answer and lets him lead her off the floor. At the

bar, as X turns toward her to find out what she wants, she speaks a very brief sentence, in which only the last word is recognizable: *soda*. X, turning toward the bartender, orders two drinks; only the beginning of his sentence is audible: *Give us two . . .*

The hubbub of the room continues, consisting of mingled, quite incomprehensible conversations, in which only occasional words can be recognized: *Really very warm in here . . . A little fresh air . . . may take a turn for the worse . . . won't do much good . . .*

They take their glasses and remain standing, silent, without even looking at each other. Both seem inattentive, lost in the crowd: it is almost as if they were not together. A drinks a little. X doesn't drink, he has even left his glass on the bar; his eyes seem to follow someone in the crowd (someone invisible). A stares into space, toward the bar or the floor; her inattentive expression is a little more disturbed than usual.

The other people around them have not really moved away, but turned in other directions, so that X and A are somewhat isolated, despite the crowd. A is seen in profile; X is quite close to, but a little behind her, and, instead of looking at her, he seems to be staring over her head, their two sight lines making a right angle, or something of the kind (X is in full face, for instance). X begins talking.

He talks in a very low but resonant voice, not whispering. His voice, instead of seeming to come from the position he occupies on the screen, is quite close: as if the character were shown in close-up. But his lips can none the less be seen pronouncing the words. His tone is that of someone who might be talking to himself, or to no one at all, describing a remote, almost indifferent recollection, though with assurance. The hubbub has considerably diminished.

X: *I met you again. —You had never seemed to be waiting for me, but we kept meeting each other at each turn in the path, behind each bush—at the foot of each statue—at the rim of every pond. It was as if only you and I had been there in that whole garden.*

Pause. There can still be heard, vaguely and without the slightest word being comprehensible, the noises of the ballroom mingled with a distinct sound of footsteps across gravel. Over this noise of footsteps, X continues:

X: *We were talking about anything that came into our heads— about the names of the statues, about the shapes of the bushes, about the water in the ponds—or else we weren't talking at all.*

Pause. Complete silence (the noises in the room have been entirely suppressed). While X talks, in a voice that is always calm, the two faces remain impassive. X seems to be seeing the garden and the scenes he is describing; A to be hearing nothing at all. Around them, as they remain motionless, other people move and shift positions, but slowly and discreetly. They seem not to notice the two protagonists, paying no attention to them.

X: *At night, most of all, you enjoyed not talking.*

Immediately there appears a very brief shot (one second?) representing an empty, bare bedroom, furnished with nothing but a single bed. It is the bedroom that will be shown later with the customary decoration and furnishings—that is, with a rather elaborate ornamentation, like all the rest of the hotel. But for the moment there are only bare walls, painted a uniformly pale color (almost white), and its only furniture this extremely narrow bed with rumpled sheets; there are no curtains at the windows and no rug on the floor. The room is filled with a very white light that resembles the brilliance of the garden more than the illumination of the hotel. Nothing can be seen through the windows.

A stands in the middle of the room, slightly to one side of the screen and in the middle distance, motionless in the pose described by X during the poker game: the tip of her bare right foot resting on the floor, her shoe in one hand; she is looking toward the camera.

But the image of the bar returns at once, just as it was a second before, with X and A, who have not moved an inch. In the silence, the sounds of two people walking side by side across gravel can be heard very distinctly. Then X, still without looking at A, speaks one more phrase.

X: *One night, I went up to your room. . . .*

And after a silence, the image of the bedroom returns. And again the bar, etc. While the large orchestra is heard tuning up, the two alternating shots—the bedroom, full of light, with A alone in the middle of the floor, and the bar with X and A, much darker— succeed each other at a rapid rhythm, each appearance of the bedroom lasting imperceptibly longer than the preceding one, while the shots of the bar, on the contrary, grow emphasized by a violent noise from the orchestra tuning up: drum roll or cymbal crash, trumpet call, etc.

The last shot of the bar is completely silent, the various instruments having finished tuning up (can the conductor's baton taps be heard?).

Finally the bedroom remains on the screen. It is still just as it was in its first appearances, but there are also two stools and a great number of pairs of shoes. A is sitting on one of the stools; the other is next to her and on it is the glass she was holding during the bar scene; on the other side of the stool she is sitting on, the shoes are spread out on the floor.

A is changing her shoes, but she is making the wrong gestures: looking for her shoes where there are none, trying to put a shoe on her left foot when it is her right foot that is bare, etc.

From the beginning of the shot, the same waltz music starts again, exactly the same but muted, a little distant, with sudden more intense bursts, like a faraway music in a garden suddenly growing lower with a gust of wind.

A looks up toward the camera, as if she heard someone coming. A kind of grin appears on her face, resembling a frozen smile. Then X appears on the screen, in the rather blurred foreground, on the opposite side from A. Dominating the music, which is very faint at this moment, A's laughter has echoed offscreen, quite recognizable, for it has often been heard already. It is cut short

when the shot changes.

Again the bar in the grand ballroom. A and X are still there, in the same place, more or less leaning against the bar. Not far from them, couples are waltzing (to the right and left, in the foreground?). A young woman is laughing (her laugh closely resembles A's, which it seems to prolong); coming from the foreground, she heads toward the bar, where A is standing: she is accompanied by two men, in a lively and relaxed little group.

X and A, on the contrary, remain frozen. X is looking at A, A is looking at the young woman laughing; she is still holding her glass. The young woman passes quite close to her to reach the bar, and stands almost behind A, very close to her.

Then A looks up at X, and immediately makes a rather sudden movement backward; but the shot is cut at this moment. During its entire duration, the waltz has been heard at its normal volume; the same is true for the following shot.

This is the bedroom again, still in the same state, with the same lighting and from the same angle. The scene is resumed at precisely the moment it had been left: A, sitting on her stool, has raised her fixed, anxious eyes to X (seen from behind or in a three-quarters view from the rear) who takes a step toward her. He is wearing the same suit as in the ballroom.

A, trying to escape, stands up abruptly and clumsily, moving backward toward the other stool, which she knocks over as well as the glass on it. The glass breaks on the floor, making a considerable noise (no doubt an abnormal one, since it even manages to drown out the music). But the image is interrupted at the breaking of the glass.

And X and A are seen again near the bar, in the ballroom. They have not moved at all, or almost not at all. X is in exactly the same position, looking impassively at A. A has stepped back a little, she must have bumped into the woman behind her. A is looking at her glass, which has fallen to the floor and broken into a thousand pieces at her feet. Other people are looking at the broken glass too, in a loose circle around her; a waiter in a white jacket is already sweeping up the pieces with a rag. The photograph should be taken near the floor so that the scattered glass is easily visible.

It would probably be best to show this in three successive shots: 1) the floor seen from above, 2) a horizontal shot showing X and A and several others, with frozen faces, 3) a new shot of the floor between people's feet.

The music has continued after a few seconds: it is the same conclusion already heard once before. Hence the version of the waltz played this time must be abridged in relation to the first version, for much less time has elapsed since the piece started, and there has been no apparent cut at any time.

The waltz over, there is silence. This time the hubbub of the room is not heard. Only faint noises are audible: the clinking of the pieces of glass the waiter is sweeping up with his rag. If the three successive shots are used, the first (broken glass on the floor) would correspond to the end of the waltz, the second (the motionless characters) to the complete silence, and the third (the broken glass the waiter is sweeping up) to the noises of the pieces of glass. This last shot lasts quite a long time.

Resembling this last shot of the broken glass on the floor, there is then a shot of a round table (the poker table) with the poker chips scattered across it, suggesting the pieces of glass in their arrangement. Selecting identical chips, M is arranging the series of his favorite game: 7, 5, 3, 1. There are two other men with him, around the table. They are standing, they have no doubt been playing poker and M is about to suggest his game to them before they separate (but this is not certain). No one says anything. Perhaps a few casual noises can be heard: chairs shifted or sounds of the same kind. It is, moreover, a brief shot: M merely begins arranging the chips.

A view of the hotel: for instance, one of the grand staircases, photographed from above. It is night, as in all the preceding scenes (dances, etc., save for the scenes in the imaginary bedroom that have the raw light of day). The lighting is rather faint, as if it were dimmed because of the late hour. There are groups standing

here and there on the steps, against the balustrade and in the hall below, generally couples. Rather brief stationary shot with a few scattered, vague noises (doors, bells . . .) unrelated to the image.

A garden view, at night. X is standing next to the stone rim of a pond. He is looking at the water, leaning slightly forward. Shadows pass around him. He is wearing the same suit as in the ballroom scene. He remains motionless for the entire length of the shot.

At the beginning this shot is entirely silent, except perhaps for a very faint sound of footsteps on the gravel when people (shadows) pass near X. The footsteps having moved off, the silence is re-established at the moment when X's voice begins again off-screen:

X's VOICE: *There were always walls—everywhere, around me— smooth, even, glazed, without the slightest relief, there were always walls . . .*

Fade: the image darkens further, then brightens again, this time showing the new image. It is a view of a corridor in the hotel, with doors and room numbers on the doors, which are closed.

The shot is not stationary: the camera advances toward a wall, turns a corner in order to continue moving, reaches a new wall, turns again, etc.

The camera continues moving slowly, steadily, zigzagging through the hotel. The course covered in this way must be extremely rich in various sequences of columns, porticoes, lobbies, little staircases, intersecting corridors, closets, etc. Moreover the labyrinth effect is increased by the presence of monumental mirrors that reflect other perspectives of complicated passageways.

There are people here and there, almost always standing still: either servants on duty, or little groups of guests in conversation, with expressions that are both banal and strange (it is probably because their words are incomprehensible that the people have strange expressions). In these groups, M is seen quite often, and A occasionally, but the camera passes over her like the others. X is never seen.

It happens that the same point is passed several times, that the same people are encountered at different points, that several routes are followed in attempting to find a way out, etc.

During the whole movement of the camera, X's voice, which has not been interrupted at the change of shots, continues off-screen.

X's VOICE: . . . and silence too. I have never heard anyone raise his voice in this hotel—no one . . . The conversations developed in the void, as if the sentences meant nothing, were intended to mean nothing in any case. And a sentence, once begun, suddenly remained in suspension, as though frozen by the frost . . . But starting over afterwards, no doubt, at the same point, or elsewhere. It didn't matter. It was always the same conversations that recurred, the same absent voices. The servants were mute. The games were silent, of course. It was a place for relaxation, no business was discussed, no projects were undertaken, no one ever talked about anything that might arouse the passions. Everywhere there were signs: Silence, Quiet.

Mingling with this speech, there can also be heard words, fragments of words, snatches of sentences (taken at random from something), but not distinctly pronounced: starting from zero, the sound increases very rapidly, attains normal volume and immediately fades (all in a second or two). There are also various sounds that have often been heard already: bells, doors, etc. The sounds of conversation should normally occur when the camera passes near a group, but the opposite is the case. Sometimes the people are behind a glass partition and nothing at all is heard.

Finally the camera reaches a group which includes X. The group appears in the background and the camera approaches until it fills the scene. Then the camera stops and the stationary shot continues until the group disperses.

There are four or five persons standing. X is at one side, a little behind, although also facing the center of the group. He takes no part in the conversation; he is content to listen.

The sound of the words starts from zero and increases while the camera approaches; but this increase is too rapid from the point of view of plausibility, and normal intensity is achieved long before the camera is through moving.

90

CHARACTER (a): *Yes, I think I remember something about it too.*

CHARACTER (b): *Still, it seems incredible.*

CHARACTER (c): *Did you see it yourself?*

CHARACTER (d): *No, but this friend of mine who told me about it . . .*

CHARACTER (c): *Oh, well . . . told you about it . . .*

These last three lines, already heard previously, must be reproduced exactly (same sound track).

CHARACTER (a): *Well it's something that's easy enough to check. You'll find all the weather reports in any file of newspapers.*

CHARACTER (d): *Let's go and look in the library.*

The group disperses. CHARACTER (d), who was on the left side of the screen, leaves toward the left, one of the others follows him; the last three leave at the rear. X remains alone, on the right side; impassively he watches them leave, then turns to the right.

The camera then moves to the right to focus on X, who, having pivoted 90 degrees, is suddenly just opposite A, who appears to have passed without seeing him (his back was to her). He stands motionless and bows politely. A, on the contrary, has instinctively recoiled upon seeing him; but she has controlled herself and stopped after taking half a step backward; she replies to X's bow with a little nod; X stares at her for a moment without speaking.

His face relaxes and it is with a smiling, innocuous expression that he begins:

X: *Do you know what I just heard? That last year at this season, it was so cold that the water in the pônds froze.*

A doesn't answer. She merely continues to meet his eyes. She is seen in a three-quarter view from behind. X is shown almost full face, smiling. Neither one moves.

Close-up of A, full face. Her face is motionless, though she seems to be struggling against something, some inner threat. This shot is of very short duration. X's voice is heard offscreen, still relaxed.

X's VOICE: *But that must be a mistake.*

Immediately: a shot of A and X in the garden. She is shown from behind, he in full face, looking at each other. They are in exactly the same place and position as in the shot of the group that concluded A's walk down the central path. X is standing, leaning against a stone balustrade. A is in the foreground, about ten feet from him; but all the rest of the group has disappeared.

A's voice is heard, somewhat altered. It is certainly the A shown on the screen who is talking, but since she is seen from behind, there is some doubt about this: the voice could be A's from the salon. A faint, hesitant voice:

A: *What is it you want from me? . . . You know very well it's impossible . . .*

Close-up of A's face, the same as in the shot before last. But now it is the imaginary bedroom that is seen behind her, instead of the hotel salon.

The shot lasts a little longer. After a moment's silence, X's voice continues, but it is no longer quite the smiling voice of the conversation in the salon.

X's VOICE: *One evening, I went up to your bedroom . . .*

Another shot of A in the imaginary bedroom: the camera has merely moved back, in relation to the preceding shot. This one now reproduces the angle of the last scene in the bedroom. The setting is virtually the same, except for certain details: the bed is made, the two stools and the shoes have disappeared; the glass, intact, is on a bed table, at the head of the bed.

A is alone, standing in the middle of the room, and looks around her with a rather bewildered expression. At the change of shot, X's voice continues his sentence, offscreen.

X's VOICE: *... You were alone ...*

But the voice stops at once, and after rather a long silence, it is A who begins talking (the character on the screen is speaking); her tone is alarmed, exasperated, almost suppliant.

A: *Let me alone ... Please ...*

The shot of the salon immediately returns, as it was before, with X and A in the same position: X almost full face, smiling, and A looking at him, turned so as to be seen in a three-quarters view from behind. She ends her sentence from the shot before, but in a more resolute tone.

A: *... Let me alone.*

X's half-smile becomes broader, as pleasant as possible, and he says, in the same conventional tone as at the beginning of the conversation:

X: *It was almost summer ... Yes, you're right. Ice ... would be out of the question.*

After a pause, he continues:

X: *But I think it's time to go to the concert. Would you allow me to accompany you?*

A answers none of X's remarks. When he suggests accompanying her, she merely makes a gesture with her head, perhaps even one without a precise meaning. And they begin walking, more or less together, X a little behind, but guiding A, even so, at a certain distance. They do not speak.

The camera follows them. There are people here and there in the background. Crossing a threshold, they find themselves in M's presence, standing alone and smoking. A stops. X continues, then stops too, at a discreet distance.

A and M, in each others' presence, remain silent at first, M looking at her, A looking a little to one side; then M says:

M: *You're going to the concert?*

This is almost not a question. A answers with a nod and says, looking at M:

A: *I'll meet you later for dinner.*

And she continues walking. X does the same; and quite natural-

ly, as if without ostentation, they find themselves walking together again.

They are now following the long gallery from the beginning of the film, but near one end, so that it does not take too long to reach the end. The angle and the camera movement must be the same as those of the initial long traveling shot. The only difference is that X and A are shown walking along the corridor; there are no other guests visible; only some motionless servants posted at certain points. This movement ends, like that of the beginning of the film, with a series of complicated passageways. But the light is more evenly distributed now: it is a normal lighting for this kind of place.

A shrill bell is heard, quite close and continuous, the kind of bell that announces the beginning of a theater performance.

After a few seconds, X's voice offscreen mingles with this bell, repeating the text from the beginning: *forever in a marble past, like these statues, this garden carved out of stone, this hotel itself with its salons empty now, its motionless characters . . .*

But the text is virtually inaudible on account of the bell. Moreover, the voice soon dies away, and the bell continues alone, always at the same volume.

The bell stops exactly as X and A enter the theater. Then there is complete silence until the beginning of the piece the orchestra plays.

This time the room is brilliantly lighted (or at least well lighted) and there are many fewer people. The seats, arranged irregularly like the first time, are for the most part unoccupied. X and A sit down, not side by side, but close to one another: A sits down first, and X takes a chair a little behind her, with an empty seat between them.

As soon as they are seated, the light in the room goes out and the camera turns toward the stage, which was already glimpsed: the musicians were already in place, motionless and ready to begin, and the spectators in the room itself already frozen, turned toward the stage. Perhaps the lighting of the stage merely increased when that of the rest of the theater went out.

It is a small orchestra; for instance: a grand piano, a flute, or a set of kettledrums, cymbals and a contrabassoon or some other ensemble that is as decorative, and rather unclassical. The conductor raises his baton. X turns to look at A, who is watching the orchestra. The orchestra begins to play.

The piece it is playing has already served as an accompaniment for certain scenes of the film since the beginning: serial music consisting of notes separated by silences, an apparent discontinuity of notes and unrelated chords. But at the same time the music is violent, disturbing and for the spectator who is not interested in contemporary music it must be both irritating and somehow continually unresolved.

The orchestra ensemble matters little. It must, none the less, use only instruments of classical music, and as much as possible those of remarkable appearance: open grand piano, harp, kettledrums, contrabassoon, slide trombone, etc.

The camera moves forward, thus eliminating A and X from the field of vision. It does not remain for long on the orchestra, whose picturesque aspect it will moreover avoid; and the shot changes, on a powerful cymbal crash. The piece comes to an end on the following shot.

The garden; reproduction of the images seen during its first appearance in the film: lateral movement of the camera showing a whole series of paths, lawns, ponds, balustrades, clipped shrubbery, statues.

But the scene is no longer empty; standing here and there, motionless as statues (but straight, arms held alongside bodies, without eccentric attitudes) are people, isolated or in couples;

if possible, there is sunlight, and the shadows of these characters are clearly visible. (Otherwise, can artificial shadows be painted for them on the ground?)

The camera does not stop moving at any one character, but continues straight and steady. At a particular moment, it reveals, almost in the foreground, X and A. They had previously been concealed by a statue. They are standing, in a vague (extremely vague) hiding place. They are not close to each other; X, his hand extended toward A, is caressing her face with his fingertips, outlining her lips and cheek. They are both serious, their heads perfectly straight; X is very calm, A slightly troubled. She murmurs:

A: *Please . . . let me alone.*

Although she is speaking in a low voice, she is heard very distinctly, for her phrase falls in a silence of the music, or on a long, soft note. But the camera passes over them like all the rest, and the progress through the garden continues without even slowing down.

The shot changes on a new cymbal crash, identical to the first (though others may have been heard in the interval), and it is the orchestra that returns: then the gesture of the cymbalist is seen continuing from the place where he had been interrupted: both arms raised, cymbals already separated, making two broad symmetrical curves in mid-air.

The piece quickly comes to an end (after several seconds); it has lasted scarcely a minute in all (less, no doubt). This return of the orchestra should be a stationary shot in which the cymbalist is clearly seen, standing at the rear, and X's face and A's in the foreground, in three-quarters.

At the end, no spectator moves, no one applauds. The musicians, too, remain frozen in their places. The conductor keeps his baton raised, watchfully.

A new shot showing, more distinctly, X and A and the people around them, all in the same position as in the preceding shot. The light is back on in the theater, but no one moves. The stage is almost or even completely invisible: the shot is taken facing it, but directed downward toward the backs of the spectators.

The light goes out again, and the orchestra begins playing the same piece again, in exactly the same way. This time, the cymbal crash produces no change of shot (it occurs either in this shot or in the next).

New shot of the theater, taken from the opposite direction (or almost), so that this time there is no question of seeing the stage. The shot reveals, head on, a group of listeners, including A, but the angle makes it impossible to see X; however the field of vision does include a number of empty seats (on either side of A, in particular). This shot is very dim; only the faces emerge from the darkness: turned toward the stage and illuminated by the light from it. Motionless and attentive faces. But A's face is quite different from the others, as though absorbed by something else: her eyes lowered, for instance, or fixed in space.

Although the piece of serial music has begun exactly the same way as the first time, and although it has remained the same as during the first hearing for a certain time (beyond the first cymbal crash), it then develops differently, for it lasts much longer, continuing, after these first two shots of the theater, through the entire first part of the following shot, which is quite long.

Fast fade: the preceding shot goes completely dark, then gradually brightens again, showing the same people seated in apparently the same order, but in another part of the hotel: in some salon. The position of the faces cannot be precisely the same, but it should sufficiently resemble the earlier one for the spectator to have the impression of seeing the paler areas appear in the same parts of the screen. A, in particular, should be at virtually the same point. X is still absent from the screen. A number of empty seats still appear, particularly on either side of A. Her face is exactly the same as in the preceding shot.

The lighting is now the normal lighting of a salon in the hotel. People are talking, but nothing of what they say can be heard. They are sitting at random and perhaps do not form any one group. It is not possible to tell whether the conversation is general. Only the concert music is heard, troubled and troubling, very violent at times.

X appears, strolling hesitantly. A is not facing him, and he does not notice her. He greets two or three people in the group, as if he were asking their permission to take a seat among them. And he sits down, but a little behind them: he does not seem to mingle much with the others. He does not speak, his expression is remote.

Finally X, turning his head, notices A's presence. She notices him too and makes a movement as if to leave the group, but X greets her with an ambiguous smile; then he continues staring at her fixedly, having resumed his grave, almost exalted expression. She gives up trying to leave. While the others continue their conversations (changing partners as well), the two of them remain looking at each other in silence.

Two people of the group get up and leave. A watches them go. Then someone else leaves the salon as well, and A seems about to imitate him, but again she meets X's eyes and remains where she is. In the most natural manner possible, everyone leaves, one after the other. People standing, who may also have been glimpsed in the vicinity, have also disappeared. There remain, finally, only X and A on the screen, at a certain distance from each other, among the empty seats, staring at each other but not seated face to face.

The music has gradually faded, the sounds becoming both more widely spaced and less violent, more discreet. When X and A are alone, it should have disappeared entirely, without its conclusion being apparent.

After looking at A for a moment in complete silence, X turns away, staring straight ahead, but his eyes lowered. And he begins talking, his voice deliberate and low, as though dreaming aloud.

X: *You never seemed to be waiting for me—but we kept meeting at each turn of the paths—behind each bush, at the foot of each statue, near each pond. It was as if there had been only you and I in all that garden.*

Short, silent close-up of A's face.

A corner of the garden: X and A, quite close together, seen from behind. For instance: A sitting on a bench and X behind her, a little to one side, staring at the same thing she is looking at: a pond or a lawn. X's voice continues, offscreen.

X's VOICE: *We were talking about anything at all; about the name of the statues, the shape of the bushes, the water in the ponds, the color of the sky. —Or else we weren't talking at all.*

After this shot, a sequence of three or four shots that are as short or even increasingly shorter, showing X and A in the garden, always from behind or in a view three-quarters from the rear, not speaking. A few low, scattered notes of the troubled music accompany them.

Another shot of the garden, concluding this sequence. X and A meet face to face, at exactly the same place and in the same position as in the shot following A's walk down the central path. They are alone, X full face, leaning back against a balustrade, and A almost from behind.

Complete immobility of both characters; then X (in the image) begins talking, while A, whose face is almost invisible be-

cause of the way she is facing) is listening to him. At first X is smiling and remote, friendly, dreamy . . .

X: *But you always stayed at a certain distance, as if on the threshold, as if at the entrance to a place that was too dark, or strange . . .*

The voice pauses before continuing in a more resolute, more precise tone.

X: *Come here.*

A hesitates an instant, then takes a step or two toward X.

Close-up of A's face (still in the garden) staring straight at the camera, motionless and tense. X's voice repeats steadily, offscreen.

X's VOICE: *Come closer.*

Then, also in close-up: X caressing A's face, as they have already been shown. They are at the foot of a statue, in a vaguely secluded place; but they are not standing very close to each other.

Moreover, after a few caresses (X has perhaps outlined her lips, an eyebrow, her cheek, her lips again), she releases herself almost without moving and murmurs the same words as the first time, though her voice is more troubled.

A: *Please . . . let me alone . . .*

Then there is silence again, as at the beginning of the shot.

Close-up of X's face, worried and tense; as soon as he appears on the screen, X begins talking, slowly. (This is still the same garden scene, as in the eight shots that follow, but the setting is scarcely visible.)

X: *Always walls, always corridors, always doors—and on the other side, still more walls.*

Close-up of A's face, staring directly into the camera, eyes wide. She listens to X's words continuing offscreen.

X's VOICE: *Before reaching you—before joining you again—you have no idea what I had to go through.*

Close-up of X's face; X is silent at first, then begins speaking again, a little faster, a little more passionately. The shot changes (on the word *garden*) without interrupting his voice.

X: *And now you are here, where I have brought you. And still you draw back.—But you are here, in this garden . . .*

Close-up of A's face, listening to X; then remaining silent, not replying, after X suddenly stopped talking.

X's VOICE: *. . . within reach of my hand, within reach of my eyes, within reach of my voice, within reach of my hand . . .*

Long silence.

Close-up of X's face, listening to A, who is invisible.

A's VOICE: *Who are you?*

Close-up of A's face, listening to X, who is invisible.

X's VOICE: *You know who I am.*

Close-up of X's face, listening to A, who is invisible.

A's VOICE: *What is your name?*

Close-up of A's face, listening to X, who is invisible.

X's VOICE: *It doesn't matter.*

This line, like the three preceding it, is surrounded by broad margins of silence.

Then, this shot continuing, A begins talking, as if in a dream at first, then almost screaming her last words. She begins by repeating, like a rather distant echo:

A: *It doesn't matter.*

Then continues, after a pause:

A: *You are like a shadow—and you're waiting for me to come closer.—Oh, let me alone . . . let me alone . . . let me alone!*

The shot lasts a few seconds before changing.

Silent close-up of X's face, the features hard and a little wild, but frozen.

General view of the theater after the piece is over. View taken toward the rear of the hall (the stage is not shown) and focused on A, alone, a little to one side, in exactly the same position and at the same place as after the end of the play. X is not in the shot. The other spectators have stood up and are gathered in little groups as at the end of the play, but there are not so many of them.

No sound of conversations or applause can be heard, nor anything else. Then X's voice, offscreen, continues the dialogue of the preceding shots, saying:

X's VOICE: *It is already too late.*

Again X and A are in the salon, as they were before the garden sequence. They are sitting a certain distance from each other, with empty seats scattered around and between them. They are not looking at each other, X is talking, without turning toward A.

X: *You had asked me not to see you again.—We did see each other, of course—the next day—or the day after, or the day after that. It may have been by accident.*

A corner of the garden. X and A together, talking, but perhaps not looking at each other. The shot could constitute the reverse angle of one of the recent views of the garden: A sitting on a bench and X standing behind and a little to one side of her; this time they are seen head on, both looking straight at the camera: faces a little fixed, strained, X's very assured, A's abashed.

X, staring into space, continues talking in the same voice, as if this were the continuation of the same scene.

X: *I told you you had to leave with me. You answered that it was impossible, of course.* (A pause.) *But you know that it is possible, and that there is nothing left for you to do, now.*

A answers, after a rather long pause:

A: *Yes . . . Maybe . . . Oh no. I don't know any more.* (A pause, then, with a kind of contained violence:) *But why me? Why does it have to be me?*

X: *You were waiting for me.*

A: *No! No . . . I wasn't waiting for you. I wasn't waiting for anyone!*

X: *You weren't waiting for anything any more. It was as if you were dead . . . That's not true! You are still alive. You are here. I see you. You remember. (Brief pause.) That's not true . . . probably. You've already forgotten everything. (Brief pause.) It's not true! It's not true! You're on the point of leaving. The door of your room is still open . . .*

A: *Why? What do you want? What else do you have to offer me?*
A long silence.

X: *Nothing. (Pause.) I have nothing to offer you.*

Very fast fade: back in the hotel salon where X and A are alone among the empty chairs, as before the garden sequence. X is still talking, his voice continuing the words of the last shot quite naturally. X is still in the same position: he has not turned to face A and he is staring into space. But A is now looking at X, or through him. X ends his sentence:

X: *And I haven't promised you anything.*

He stops, continuing after a long silence, as though lost in the images he is describing.

X: *Remember . . . It was evening, probably the last one. It was almost dark. A faint shadow was advancing slowly through the darkness . . . Long before being able to distinguish the features of your face, I knew it was you.* (A pause.) *When you recognized me you stopped . . . We stood like that, a few yards from each other, without saying a word.* (A pause.) *You were standing in front of me, waiting perhaps—as if you couldn't take another step, or turn back either. You stood there, straight, motionless, your arms alongside your body.* (A pause.) *And you look at me; your eyes are wide open, too wide, your lips parted a little, as if you were going to speak, or groan, or scream . . .* (A pause.) *You are afraid.*

A has gradually assumed the expression X has described immediately afterward: frozen and limp at the same time, lips parted, eyes almost staring. After having said *You are afraid,* X slowly turns his head toward A and continues staring at her for an instant before continuing. And he is still looking at her fixedly as

he begins talking again, with an increasing although controlled ardor.

X: *Your lips part a little more, your eyes widen still further, your hand is extended in front of you in an incompleted gesture of expectation, of uncertainty, or perhaps of appeal or defense. Your fingers are trembling a little . . . You are afraid.* (A pause.) *You are afraid.*

The camera, on X's last words, makes a kind of circular movement around A in order to show her in detail; A must constantly be shown from a little above (at the height of a person standing).

Then the camera rises until, X and A being in the foreground, M is suddenly revealed between them—that is, centered but in the middle distance, and perhaps even farther away. No one moves. M smiles ambiguously but fleetingly, then assumes a more ceremonious expression.

M takes several steps toward them, that is, toward the camera, but stops at a certain distance, still watches them, seems to change his mind and merely makes a polite bow before walking off to one side.

M has disappeared, but the angle of the shot remains the same, that is, focused on the place where M was standing. The other two are still staring in this direction, where there is nothing left to see but an element of baroque architecture or of elaborate decoration which M's body was concealing a moment before. X begins talking again, still staring at this empty setting.

X: *He's the one you're afraid of.* (A pause.) *He's the one you think is watching you without being seen, he's the one who suddenly appears before you.* (A pause.)

A slowly turns her head to one side, the side away from X, that is, toward the edge of the screen, as if she were staring at something outside the field of vision, and she remains in that position for several seconds.

X: *Who is he? Your husband perhaps. —He was looking for you, or else he just happened to be passing. He was already coming toward you.* (A pause.)

X turns toward A and continues to look at her as he talks and

108

as she gradually returns to her original position: until she is staring again at the baroque setting, at the place where M was standing previously.

X: *But you remained frozen, cut off, absent . . . He didn't seem to have recognized you at first. —And he stepped forward. Something in you escaped him. —Another step. —Your eyes looked through him . . .* (A pause.) *He decided to go away . . .* (A pause.) *And now you are still staring into space . . . And you still see him . . . his gray eyes, his gray silhouette, and his smile.* (A pause.) *And you are afraid.*

After saying *looked through him,* X looks in the same direction too. Then, on the following words, A slowly stands up, while continuing to stare at the place where M was previously standing.

On the *And you are afraid,* the shot suddenly cuts to the imaginary bedroom. The modifications in this room, in relation to its last appearance on the screen, are as follows: there is now a baroque mantelpiece, skillfully integrated with the general ornamentation of the walls. There is a real fireplace, a glass identical to the one that was broken is on the mantel: it is half full of a pale liquid. (A second, similar glass is still on the night table, with half an inch of the same liquid in it.) There is a large mirror in a complicated frame over the fireplace (also, and even more important, a mirror that comes from a salon of the hotel and has already been seen several times).

A is alone, sitting on the bed (which is made up), her hands resting on the spread on either side of her body (arms slightly

spread). She is looking at the floor, a few yards in front of her, without moving. The first seconds of the shot are silent, then X's voice resumes, offscreen, continuing the speech of the preceding shot quite naturally.

X's VOICE: *It is his coming here again that you are afraid of, or his presence here already, when I come again into your bedroom.*

A rather long silence. Then the voice continues offscreen.

X's VOICE: *He stayed in an adjoining room, separated from yours by a private sitting room.*

The voice speaks imperceptibly faster, more tensely, less well controlled. These characteristics develop during the following sentences until they produce an excited and choppy tone, which then gradually grows calm again.

X's VOICE: *At that hour, in any case, he is at the gambling table. —I had warned you I would come. You didn't answer. —When I came, I found all the doors ajar: the door to the vestibule of your apartment, the door to the little sitting room, the door to your bedroom. —I only had to push them open, one after the other, and to close them again, one after the other, behind me.*

During the last phrase, A gradually looks up and turns her face toward the camera, in silence.

The silence continues during a close-up of A's face, frozen by an evident anguish. Then after a few seconds, X's voice, calm, low, but authoritative, says offscreen:

X's VOICE: *You already know the rest.*

After a moment more of immobility, A's features are distorted, her mouth gradually opens, and A begins screaming; the sound is

strident, but it has scarcely time to be produced when it is drowned out by a very close violent detonation that stops it short. Afterwards, in the silence, a regular series of identical gunshots follows, those already heard in the shooting gallery.

Face strained, mouth open, A remains motionless until the end of the shot, while the gunshots continue one after the other.

Abruptly, with the last pistol shot, a new image: the marksmen lined up in the shooting gallery, backs to the targets and facing the camera, holding the pistols alongside their bodies. M is in the row (but not X), in an easily seen place. All are motionless, waiting for the signal. Only the ticking of a clockwork mechanism is heard, rapid and distinct, throughout.

Another image showing X and A in a salon of the hotel; but they are no longer in the same place as before the bedroom scene. They are sitting alone in the same sort of position as before, not looking at each other, and with more empty seats near them; but it is not the same salon.

As soon as the image appears, A begins speaking: she is tense, agitated, she protests with a kind of anxiety.

A: *No, no, no!* (The first word is spoken quite low, then the tone rises.) *No, I don't know what happened then. I don't know you. I don't know that room, that ridiculous bed, that fireplace with its mirror . . .*

X (turning toward her): *What mirror? What fireplace? What did you say?*

A: *Yes . . . I don't know any more . . . It's all wrong . . . I don't know any more . . .*

Another part of the hotel, quite different (no empty chairs, in

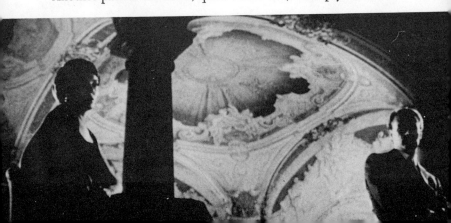

particular) but still deserted. The conversation continues with the following line spoken by X, which seems to continue from the preceding shot.

X: *If it was wrong, why are you here?* (He has resumed his calm and objective voice.) . . . *What was that mirror like?*

A's answer is on a different view of the hotel, but one quite like the first, and still deserted. X and A are still sitting at a certain distance from one another. In the background, a servant-statue, at attention.

A is speaking, her eyes staring into space; her delivery is a little choppy, her tone vague. X listens to her, staring at her fixedly now (but not into her eyes, since she is looking somewhere else).

A: *There is no mirror over the fireplace.* (She is talking as if in a dream.) . . . *It is a painting: a landscape, I think . . . a landscape with snow. The mirror is over the chest . . . There is also a dressing table with a mirror.* (A pause). *And other furniture too, of course . . .* (She stops.)

The shot changes after a moment of silence, and the conversation continues, in still another part of the hotel. X and A are standing this time, moving, walking through a salon; but their movement is quite uncertain, they are not in step, so that the distance between them is variable (and always considerable); their progress is irregular, interrupted by pauses, detours, hesitations; still they take the same way on the whole and, moreover, the spectator

112

should have the impression that it is X who guides their course. The conversation continues, from place to place, interrupted by silences.

The camera accompanies the couple in its movement. This lasts a long time, their course is a long one through the hotel: salons, corridors, doors, stairs, doors, more salons, more halls and passageways. Everything seems quite deserted; none the less there are people here and there: servants and guests too, in little groups; the servants are frozen, like sentinels posted along the route; the guests are almost always on the edge of the screen, in the background in relation to the couple's progress, generally standing in two's or three's, rather rigid too, but turning to stare impassively after A (or X). When X and A pass near a group, they stop talking and resume their dialogue a little farther on. And their route continues, slow and irregular, always seeming on the point of stopping altogether. X precedes A by a few steps, then turns toward her to wait for her; when they walk through doors, he steps back to let her pass through first, then walks a few steps ahead. The impression is that this progress leads nowhere.

Finally they reach the large entrance lobbies, the more imposing colonnades. But the spectator must not see what the view is from the bay windows, if there is any at all. A is also not to look beyond the place where she is, and this detail is to be justified by the arrangement of the setting and A's movements. None the less the lighting has probably brightened, as if the daylight outside were nearer now.

X: *And what kind of bed?*

A: *A double bed, probably* . . . (She has spoken mechanically, as if in a dream.)

X: *And what was the view from the windows?*

A: *I don't know . . . The windows . . .* (Then, a sudden awakening.) *I don't know what bedroom you're talking about. I've never been in any bedroom with you.*

A silence. They continue on their way.

X: *You don't want to remember . . . Because you're afraid.*

At this moment they are close to each other, in a narrow pas-

113

sageway. X stretches out his hand in front of A, half barring her way. She stops and looks down at X's arm in front of her.

X (gently): *Don't you recognize this bracelet either?*

He turns his hand over and opens it: a little bracelet—a simple strand of pearls just long enough to encircle a slender wrist—is shown in his hand. A looks at it, then looks away, perhaps a little troubled.

A: *Yes . . . No . . . I used to have a bracelet like that once.*

They continue walking, first in silence, then they resume their desultory conversation.

X: *And what happened to it?*

A: *I don't know. I must have lost it.*

X: *Long ago?*

A (after a hesitation): *I don't remember any more.*

They stop again, in a passageway.

X (his voice still gentle): *It was last year. And you didn't lose it. You left it with me . . . as a pledge. Your name is engraved on the clasp.*

A: *Yes. I saw it . . . But it's the most ordinary sort of name. And all pearls look alike . . . Bracelets like that . . . there must be hundreds of them . . .*

X: *Let's say it was yours then, and that I found it.*

114

He hands A the bracelet; she takes it as if to look at it more closely, but glances at it quite absently and then keeps it in her hand: one finger stuck through it and the rest held in her palm. At the same time, they have continued walking in silence. Then X begins talking again, in a lower voice—his visionary voice.

X: *I remember that room very well . . . where you were waiting for me. Yes, there was a mirror over the chest; and it was in that mirror that I saw you first, when I opened the door without making a sound . . .*

He stops for a moment, before continuing, with mounting passion.

X: *You were sitting on the edge of the bed, in a kind of robe or bed-jacket . . . it was white. I remember that you were all in white, and that you had white slippers too, and this bracelet.*

A: *No . . . no! You're making it up . . . I'm sure you're making it up . . . I've never had a white robe. You can see it must be someone else . . .*

X: *If you say so.*

A silence. After a few steps, X continues, still in the same calm and impassioned voice.

X: *But I remember that bedroom very well . . . and that white lace spread you were lying on, on the double bed.*

A (with a kind of terror): *No! Be still. Please. You're completely mad.* (A short silence.)

X (gently): *No, no, please . . . I hear your voice the way it sounded then. You were afraid. You were already afraid.*

A silence. They walk down the hall as if A were fleeing X, who is in pursuit:

X: *You've always been afraid. But I loved your fear that evening.* (Without losing its softness, his tone gradually becomes more excited.) *I watched you, letting you struggle a little . . . I loved you. There was something in your eyes, you were alive . . . finally . . . I took you, half by force.*

A has just reached the threshold of a last passageway, no

115

doubt a rather monumental one. She has turned toward X, who has remained behind her in the hall, and she takes her last steps backward, terrified by his wild tone. X, who had stopped, walks toward her again, on the words *by force;* she turns around to run away, takes one step toward the door, while he, motionless again, speaks the last words in an almost relieved tone of voice:

X: . . . *at the beginning . . . remember . . .* (A pause.) *Oh no . . . Probably it wasn't by force . . .* (The end of the phrase may be heard offscreen.) *But you're the only one who knows that.*

The camera, which has pivoted to follow the fugitive, suddenly reveals the whole garden—the garden *à la française,* which has been seen in imagination since the beginning—at the same time that A herself discovers it.

X, who has remained behind, is now outside the field of vision. A, shown from behind, advances slowly along the terrace, toward the balustrade, the statues, the regular lawns and geometric shrubs. Brilliant sunshine would be preferable here. As though dazzled by this sun, A raises one hand to her eyes, then

continues walking slowly to the balustrade. She is still seen from behind. She rests her hand on the stone balustrade, assuming precisely the pose in which the camera showed her, in this same spot, the first time. Then she turns her head, as before, but continues the movement, embracing the garden in a panoramic gaze.

The serial music already heard throughout the scene (especially in the concert scenes) now resumes, but imperceptibly: very low at first, a few scattered notes, then gradually acquiring volume, but without achieving its earlier violence. Slightly troubled music, but none the less indicating—by its arbitrary and atonal character, its sudden shrill notes, its abrupt jumps—the shock that the discovery of the garden represents: a kind of expected and therefore reassuring shock. This music continues into the following shot.

Slow panorama of the garden, as it has already been seen throughout the film. A is no longer in the field of vision. The entire garden is empty, without a guest or a servant in it. Alone, down one path, a gardener bent over his rake, in the distance no doubt.

The movement of the camera stops on A still leaning on the balustrade, full face this time. She passes her hand in front of her eyes again. Behind her we see the hotel, the façade already shown in a print; it is a shot of the garden (A walking down the long, straight path).

A in the same position, but at closer range, in the foreground. Behind her, X walks forward on the gravel. He joins her beside the balustrade and turns toward her as she shelters her eyes. They exchange a few lines, the words faint, spoken almost in an undertone, without tension; hoarse, almost broken voices. The music continues, mingled with the sounds of footsteps and the words.

X: *What is it?*

A: *Nothing . . .*

X: *Are you tired?*

A: *A little . . . Yes . . . I think so . . .*

X: *It's a . . .*

A (interrupting him): *The sun . . . all of a sudden . . .*

X: *Would you like to go in?*

A: *If you would.*

They turn around and walk toward the hotel, which is quite near. They are shown from behind, at a certain distance from each other, X slightly behind A. In a rather fast though unhurried scene, A twists her right ankle and stops. X approaches her and offers her his arm. She leans on it to take off her shoe and remains with her right foot resting on its toe, as in her first appearance in the bedroom. She is examining the broken shoe. Neither one speaks. Then X turns around toward the camera and the shot changes.

Shot of the statue already described and shown several times in the film. Stationary shot, taken at a distance, as if it was what X saw when he turned around. The music becomes more violent.

Card players in a hotel salon at night. There are seven or eight men sitting around a table, and each has several cards (face down on the table) in front of him. X and M are among the players. No one moves. The game they are playing is not specified. Fixed faces.

New shot of X and A dancing the waltz, among other couples. Attitude still as correct, but their faces, A's in particular, are clearly more dramatic, although also fixed.

The same serial music, very violent now, maintaining its choppy, discontinuous character, full of sudden silences. Consequently the dancers' movements have no relation to the rhythms heard.

A wanders, alone, through several salons of the hotel, with people in groups here and there; she seems a little forlorn, but her expression is still impassive, agreeable.

Another card table (without X): M is dealing cards, one by one, to a circle of five or six players. Fixed faces. M's rapid gestures are mechanically repeated throughout the entire shot.

Abrupt cut to X and A in a *tête-à-tête* in a corner of the garden. But no doubt there is no sunshine. The setting and the attitudes have already been seen before: for instance, A is sitting on

a bench and X standing behind her, slightly to one side. The camera reveals them at a considerable distance and gradually approaches with a regular movement. It stops when they are in the foreground (still seen from behind). It is at this moment that X begins talking, his slow voice interrupted with pauses and silences. But his mouth is not shown, nor is A's (though the words are heard as if they were being spoken facing the spectator).

X: *It was on that day you gave me the little white bracelet.* (A pause.) *And you asked me to allow you a year, thinking perhaps that you would test me that way ... or wear me out ... or forget me.* (A pause.) *But time, time doesn't count. I've come, now, to take you away.* (A silence.)

A (her voice broken and low): *No ... no ...*

The shot changes immediately after the second *no*.

Now the couple is shown from in front, in the same place, the same position, as they appeared during the last long conversation in the garden. X's face is severe, resolute, a little exalted. His hands are clutching the back of the bench. A, on the contrary, is slightly somnambulistic.

During their conversation, X sometimes looks toward the camera, his eyes raised, sometimes toward A, lowering his eyes (he can see her profile, since he is not precisely behind her, but slightly to one side). A, on the contrary, never looks at X (which is natural, since he is above and behind her), nor at the camera in front of her, save for brief glances when she turns her head wildly. She gazes only at the ground, or to the right or left. She begins to talk in the first images of the shot, continuing the same dialogue, but in a quicker, less uncertain manner:

A: *No, no. It's impossible.*

X (very gently): *No, no. It's impossible....* (He has repeated these words as if in a dream.) *Naturally.* (A pause.) *But you know very well that it is possible, that you are ready, that we're going to leave.*

A: *What makes you so sure?* (A pause.) *Leave for where?*

X (gently): *Anywhere ... I don't know.*

120

A: *You see. We'd better not see each other any more ... ever ...*
Last year ... Oh no, it's impossible. You're going to leave by
yourself ... and then we'll be ... forever. ...

X (more violently as he interrupts her): *That's not true! It's not*
true that we need absence, solitude, waiting forever. It's not
true. But you're afraid!

On the word *afraid,* the shot abruptly changes:

View of the bedroom painted and decorated as it was the last
time. Above the fireplace, instead of the mirror, there is an old

painting representing a snowy landscape. There is also a chest
(in the same style as the night table that was already in the
room) and a mirror hanging above it. Lastly, the bed is no longer
the little divan, but an enormous double bed, in the same style
and of the same wood as the rest of the furniture. The entire
setting is bare and orderly (the bed made up with its spread and
pillows, etc.) A is not in the room. It is likely that, in this stationary shot, the rest of the furniture cannot be seen, the mirrored
dressing table, for instance.

There is complete silence, until a kind of low cry uttered by
A, still invisible, on which the shot changes:

A's VOICE: *No!*

Cut back to the garden: X and A (sitting on the bench), seen
from behind, in the foreground, as before. They are quite motionless, looking straight ahead, in the same direction. X answers,
slowly, in a low voice with incoercible fervor.

121

X: *But it is too late, now.*

On X's last word, the shot changes again, abruptly: new appearance of the bedroom, virtually the same as it was just before. But now there are carpets, and the furniture, though remaining the same, has been shifted somewhat; it is apparent that everything is now in its right place and that a moment before it was not. A few additional elements complete the ensemble (chairs and various objects). The angle is the same, there is still no one in the shot; the shot lasts longer than the first time.

There is silence until the *no* that ends the shot, spoken by A offscreen, but with much less force: the final denial of someone who surrenders, as if she were saying *"For pity's sake!"*

A's VOICE: *No!*

Cut back to the garden: X and A still in the same place and in the same position, but seen full face. They are both staring fixedly at the camera. A looks completely distraught. X is filled with a kind of impassive madness (above all, no grimaces!). They say nothing. Nothing else can be heard.

Fast fade to the bedroom, exactly as it was the time before. The angle is also the same, at least at the start, for this shot is not stationary: the camera rotates to show the room in detail, and soon reveals A herself, standing and staring toward the camera, her eyes staring fixedly, looking just as upset as she had in the garden during the preceding shot. She is wearing a rather elegant dress and the slender pearl bracelet that she nervously tugs at from time to time, at the risk of breaking it. As soon as she appears on the screen, or shortly afterwards, she begins taking a few uncertain steps.

She moves hesitantly in one direction after another, as though caught in a trap. The camera follows her closely. A moves first toward a door, but stops before reaching it, moves to another door, extends her hand toward the knob, but without quite touching it, turns back and finds herself in front of a mirror, looks at herself in passing, follows one wall to the window, passes her hand in front of her face with the same gesture she made in the garden to shelter her eyes from the sun. (The shot is taken so as not to reveal what can be seen from the window.) The window is closed.

When A has started walking, X's voice is heard offscreen, completely calm and objective again, though it seems to be concealing something.

X's VOICE: *He had just gone out.* (A pause.) *I don't know what violent scene might have occurred between you, a moment before....*

Then the voice stops, while A continues wandering around the bedroom. The shot ends when she reaches the window and makes the gesture with her hand.

View of the garden from the bedroom window, with the window frame in the foreground. A is not visible, or else she is very blurred, to one side. The garden, which can be seen quite broadly, is empty, with the exception of two tiny characters alone in the center of a vast, bare expanse; they are X and A (as well as can be judged from so far away), walking side by side, at a certain distance from each other.

Reprise of the image that ended the shot before last: A seen from a certain distance looking out of her closed window (the garden is not seen from this angle). She passes her hand before her eyes, repeating the same gesture again. Then she turns around and begins walking slowly and uncertainly around the room once more, the camera following her closely as before, while X's voice resumes, offscreen.

X's VOICE: *From the window of your bedroom, you can see the garden.* (Pause.) *But you didn't see him leave, which would certainly have reassured you....*

A long silence, then the voice continues:

X's VOICE: *Then you turned back toward the bed ... undecided at first, not knowing where to go ... you turned back toward the bed, you sat down on it, then you let your body fall back and you ... you went back toward the bed ... after having*

remained undecided a few seconds—maybe even a few minutes, not knowing what to do, staring straight ahead of you into space. And you turned back toward the bed.... Oh, listen to me ... remember.... Listen to me, please.... Yes.... There was ... Yes, it's true, there was a big mirror just beside

the door, an enormous mirror you didn't dare go near, as if
it frightened you. . . . But you insist on pretending not to be-
lieve me. Where are you? Where have you gone? Why always
try to escape? It's too late. . . . It was already too late. There
was no more. . . . The door was closed now. No! No! The
door was closed. . . . Listen to me. . . .

This text is spoken in a voice that is sometimes insistent and
imperative, sometimes hesitant or irritated, sometimes frankly
suppliant, constantly repeating the directions A refuses to follow:
as if she kept as far as possible from the bed, in a kind of stubborn and unreasonable resistance. The allusion to the mirror
represents, on the contrary, a concession by X, when A looks too
long toward the mirrors (which in fact she walks toward). And
it is when she is quite close to the now open door that he speaks
the last sentences, in a desperate struggle against the images
seen on the screen. It is the bedroom door; and it is on this image
that the shot changes.

A fade: another salon of the hotel. A is alone, reading, among
empty armchairs. It is the same image as the one in which A
was already reading the first time. But she no longer has her
calm, blank expression of the beginning of the film: she is anxious, nervous, troubled. Moreover, she is not really reading: she
is absently leafing through a few pages of her book; then she
looks up, turns toward the camera, and remains in this position
a moment; then, abruptly, she looks in the opposite direction
(almost behind her), as if she had heard someone. But there
is no one, she returns to her book, picks it up, lays it on her
lap, etc.

Then X's voice is heard once again: this time it is very calm,
having completely recovered the tone of the most objective
narrative.

X's VOICE: *What proof do you still need?* (A pause.) *I had also*
kept a photograph of you, taken one afternoon in the park, a
few days before you left. But when I gave it to you, you
answered, again, that it proved nothing. Anyone could have
taken the snapshot, at any time, and anywhere: the setting
was vague, remote, scarcely visible. . . .

On these last words the book slips from her lap and falls to the floor, a photograph drops out of it. A leans down and, after looking at it, puts the photograph back between the pages of the book, which she replaces on her lap. Then, thinking better of it, she picks up the book, leafs through it, finds the photograph again and looks at it more carefully (she also looks at the back of the photograph). It is a photograph of herself, in a garden. After an interruption, the voice continues, offscreen.

X's VOICE: *A garden . . . Any garden . . . I would have had to show you the white lace spread, the sea of white lace where your body . . . But all bodies look alike, and all white lace, all hotels, all statues, all gardens. . . .* (A pause.) *But this garden, for me, looked like no other one. . . . Every day, I met you here. . . .*

The shot changes while A is looking at the photograph.

Close-up of the photograph, enlarged to the dimensions of the screen, so that it is no longer evident that it is a candid snapshot. It is, moreover, a real shot and not a stationary photograph, but since A remains motionless in it, it is scarcely (or not at all) apparent that the image is animated. The face is seen head on, staring at the camera, relaxed and smiling, in an atmosphere of vacation· pleasures. The voice offscreen continues.

X's VOICE: *A quiet place, with few people in it, often deserted in fact; particularly during the hot part of the day . . . in summer . . .*

The image suddenly changes: it is now a profile close-up of X and A staring at each other, but a certain distance apart. X is talking. A begins to smile, almost to laugh, completely relaxed. Between the two can be seen a long perspective of gardens (still the same gardens).

This shot is at first silent. Although X's lips are moving in the shot, and though he is evidently talking, nothing can be heard; similarly A's laughter is quite mute. And it is X's voice offscreen that continues at this moment.

X's VOICE: *. . . It was an afternoon. . . .* (The voice is a little uncertain.) *the next day, probably. . . . I had just told you we would be leaving. . . . But you weren't laughing. . . .* (The voice is firmer now.) *That we would be leaving the next morning, a ride in my car would be our excuse . . . but we would never come back . . .* (The voice more uncertain again.) *while he . . .*

The shot changes in the middle of A's laughter, which has begun again, though still soundless.

Close-up of A laughing, full face—identical, in setting, distance and angle, to the photograph that dropped out of the book as it appeared in the shot before last. Only A's expression has changed. X's voice offscreen fades into uncertainty:

X's VOICE: *. . . while he . . . No . . . That wasn't it . . .*

Another shot of X and A talking in the garden. This time they are shown from farther away, and the immediate setting around them is easier to see: it is a characteristic corner of the park showing, in particular, and quite close to them, the statue

already seen and described at some length (the one with two figures) and which none the less certainly was not in this location the other times.

As in the two preceding shots, A seems to have lost both her "vacuum" from the beginning of the film and her anxiety of the last scenes. By her attitudes and her face (the words are unknown), she seems merely beautiful and relaxed, perhaps a little excited.

Here again the dialogue of the visible characters is replaced by the offscreen voice which, after a rather long silence, speaks the rest of its choppy, hesitant narrative.

X's VOICE: *Yes, we were in your bedroom.... Our departure must already have been set the day before.... You had agreed ... reluctantly, perhaps ...* (A pause.) *I was in your bedroom. ...* (Pause.) *From the door, it is the bed you see first....*

Then the camera gradually moves back and, if possible, higher. The characters thus have an increasingly broad garden area around them; but the statue on its base, because of its location, seems on the contrary to grow larger in relation to them. The voice does not stop.

X's VOICE: *But the dressing table wasn't visible from the threshold. ... You were probably standing on the opposite side of the room, near the window, looking out at the garden, perhaps.... I don't remember any more exactly....* (A pause.) *On the stairs, I had passed him going down.... He had just*

left your bedroom. . . . Unless that was another day. . . . (A pause.) That evening everything was empty: stairs, corridors, stairs. . . .

Then, abruptly, the characters disappear, whisked out of the image. At the same time the shot becomes stationary again and lasts some seconds this way, fixed on the empty garden and its statue.

The voice is cut short, at the very moment when the two characters disappear from the image, by the first (rather loud) note of serial music (of the type heard frequently before), rather soft here and with numerous gaps of silence. This music will continue into the following shot, with the same characteristics, and with occasional abrupt and violent climaxes, as irritating as possible.

And suddenly the bedroom returns again, in precisely the state in which it was left (setting, furnishings and various accessories). A is standing in the middle, at the same place and in the same position as when the camera revealed her previously, her eyes fixed and anxious, nervously tugging at her slender pearl bracelet. Almost immediately she breaks the bracelet. The pearls drop to the floor. She squats or kneels on the carpet to pick them up. She is now in a rather severe housecoat (which is not the white robe which has already been referred to). Her expression is again troubled, anxious; and she shows the same signs of expectation, or fear, as in the recent scene where she was leafing through a book in the reading room.

During a rather soft passage of the music, X's voice is heard again, increasingly nonplussed, offscreen:

X's VOICE: *He had come in. . . . You had been surprised by his visit. . . . He didn't seem to have any specific purpose. He referred to the concert of the night before, I think . . . or else it was you who began talking first. . . . No . . . No . . . I don't remember any more. . . . I don't remember any more myself.* (A pause, then in a very weary voice.) *I don't remember any more.*

A stands up, sets the pearls on the chest, looks at the floor again, raises her eyes, glances in various directions—toward the doors, the mirrors, into space. She crosses the bedroom to look out the window and, as if she were trying to see something just at the foot of the wall outside, stands on tiptoe, looking straight down. Then she goes to her dressing table, turns back toward the window, but without doing whatever she had intended, takes several irresolute steps and returns to the dressing table, where she sits down for a second, but immediately stands up again, etc.

During this interval, the camera itself has given certain signs of agitation: executing various rotations, reversals, and even sudden changes of shot.

On one of these abrupt changes, A appears again near the window, looking down, through the panes that are in her way. Nothing of what she sees appears; perhaps nothing at all can be seen beyond the panes, because of the way in which the shot is taken.

The music has stopped, as if one of the gaps in the score were continuing indefinitely; hence the beginning of the shot is completely silent. Then a knocking at the door is heard, clear and discreet the first time, a little louder the second time.

Hearing someone knock, A turns around quickly; remaining motionless at first, straining to hear, she then walks noiselessly across the carpet toward the dressing table. More knocking while she sits down; still not answering, she picks up her hairbrush and begins brushing her hair. At the sound of the door opening, she looks to one side, toward the mirror over the chest. Immediately the shot changes to show the other side of the room.

M, who has just come in, stands motionless in front of the bedroom door that he has already closed behind him. He is in evening dress, smiling, ceremonious, a little distant but attentive. He walks slowly forward across the room as he speaks. Occasionally he looks at A, who is carefully brushing her hair so as not to have to look at M.

M approaches the chest, and A's photograph is seen on top of it: it is the photograph which was in the book (the size of a postcard). He picks it up and looks at it a moment, while continuing to talk. He does not seem to attach much importance to it, but his tone throughout the entire conversation, should be somewhat ambiguous: is this an interrogation or not? A is absorbed in brushing her hair, which partly conceals her nervousness. Then M goes to the window; he barely glances out of it and returns toward A, etc. He makes all these movements quite casually and yet there is a kind of precision in his gestures, as if each step were calculated; his movements in the room are as different as possible in character from A's just before he came in.

The camera, too, makes much less jerky movements. Moreover they are slow and of small scope, their only goal being to keep both M and A in the field of vision; as much as is possible, A should remain in the background in relation to M.

M begins talking almost at once. The conversation is desultory, as if they were "elsewhere."

M: *I knocked. . . . Didn't you hear?*

A: *Of course. I told you to come in.*

M: *Oh . . . You couldn't have said it very loud.*

A silence. He looks at the photograph.

M: *What's this photograph?*

A: *What it looks like . . . an old picture of me.*

M: *Yes.* (A pause.) *When was it taken?*

A: *I don't know . . . Last year?*

M: *Oh.* (A pause.) *Who took it?*

A: *I don't know. . . . Frank, maybe . . .*

M: *Last year, Frank wasn't here.*

A silence.

A: *Well, maybe it wasn't taken here. . . . It might have been Frederiksbad. . . . Or else it was someone else.*

A pause.

M: *Yes . . . probably.* (A pause.) *What did you do with your afternoon?*

A: *Nothing . . . I read. . . .*

M: *I looked for you. . . . Were you in the park?*

A: *No, in the green room . . . near the theater.*

M: *Oh, there . . . But I passed through there.* (A pause.)

A: *Did you have something to tell me?*

M: *No.* (A pause. Gently, a little sadly:) *You look upset.*

A: *I'm a little tired. . . .*

A has begun looking at the floor again, beside her, where the pearls might have rolled when she broke the bracelet. M watches her.

M: *You should get some rest. Don't forget, that's why we're here.* (A pause.) *Did you lose something?*

A: *No . . . Maybe some pearls. I broke my little bracelet.*

M: (looking at the pearls on the chest): *That's not serious. . . . You know they're false.*

A: *Yes . . .*

But she continues looking, her face lowered. M starts for the door. Then she glances up.

A: *You're leaving?*

M: *I think I'll go to the shooting gallery.*

M has stopped near the door he came in at the beginning of the scene.

A: *At this hour?*

M: *Yes. Why not?* (A pause.) *Anderson is coming tomorrow. . . . We'll have lunch with him at noon . . . if you have no other plans. . . .*

A: *No . . . of course not . . . what plans?*

M: *Until this evening, then.*

The shot is cut when M opens the door to leave.

The camera follows the same scene from a new angle, focused on A now, in the foreground. While M leaves (but he is not shown on the screen), A pretends to be absorbed in brushing her hair. As soon as the sound of the door closing is heard, she stands up, without leaving her place in front of the dressing table, her ear turned toward the door through which M has just left. After a few seconds of complete immobility, she takes two or three steps toward the center of the room, stiff and irresolute at the same time, her eyes staring into space. She glances briefly at the window; then, still turned toward the window, she looks down at the floor and remains in this position for several seconds, as though absorbed in some difficult reflection, more vacant than agonized, staring at her hand, perhaps, half-extended in front of her in a gesture which might reproduce for instance that of a statue seen in the park (and her housecoat, too, might suggest such a thing).

A long silence follows M's departure, then the voice begins

again offscreen, rather low at first, but having recovered its assurance, its regular delivery, its objective tone, and soon achieving its normal intensity.

X's VOICE: *Once the door was closed again, you listened for the sound of footsteps in the little sitting room that separates your bedrooms, but you could hear nothing, and you didn't hear any other noises of doors either.* (Brief silence.) *The easiest way to the shooting gallery was the terrace along the rear façade of the hotel.* (Brief silence.) *But without opening the window, you couldn't see this area, located at the foot of the wall. You hoped to hear the sound of his footsteps on the gravel; it was scarcely possible, from this height, through the panes; moreover there is probably no gravel there anyway.*

On the words *there anyway* she suddenly turns toward the door, raising her eyes to the height of a man's eyes; and the shot immediately changes to show what she sees.

The shot is centered on the door, already closed, by which X has just come in. The image this produces is exactly that of M's arrival: a motionless man standing in front of the door, facing the camera; but it is X now, and not M. He gives a brief, strange smile, almost a madman's smile, and his eyes are mad.

Reverse angle: A making signs to X to be still, to be careful, to be on guard against an imminent danger; she seems quite beside herself; she is still wearing the same housecoat, but it seems transformed: less austere, much more seductive. This shot is quite rapid. A must be at one side of the screen, and not in the middle.

Sudden change of shot: the same room, but taken toward the window; if there are several windows, it is always the same one that must be used: the one through which A and later M have looked out; now it is seen again, with M in front of it in the same position as that which he occupied to look outside a moment ago— that is, against the light and from behind. He is in the center of the screen, and no one else is shown. He turns around in a single movement, raising an arm in front of him: he has a pistol in his hand and he fires immediately (exactly the same movement as in the shooting gallery). Rapid image, which is cut as soon as the pistol, pointed toward the camera, has fired.

The detonation is not heard (or else it is a very distant, faint sound); yet the smoke coming out of the barrel is visible.

Then an extremely rapid shot of A's body stretched out on the floor, seen from above. Her eyes are wide open and her mouth parted, a kind of ecstatic expression on her face. Her dress, half open, is now frankly provocative. Her hair is loose, in a disorder that is also very seductive. She has fallen onto a thick fur rug (was it there before?).

Abrupt change of shot: X and A in a salon of the hotel, sitting in some secluded corner, in the same position they have often been seen in already: relatively distant from and not looking at each other; but the setting is probably not the same as for the preceding conversations. Between X and A, standing a certain distance away and looking toward them, is M, in exactly the posture of the scene where he had approached and then withdrawn without saying anything.

X and A are seen full face in the foreground, and M farther back, also facing the camera. On the initial image, M should be distinctly closer to A than to X (it is a question of the apparent distance, on the screen). But the shot is not stationary: it oscillates, from the moment it appears. Centered first on X-A(it shifts toward A, until it is centered on M-A (X is out of the field of vision at this moment), then it returns toward X until it is centered on him (then M and A are outside the field of vision), finally it returns toward A and stops when it is centered, as at the beginning, on X-A. But M has now disappeared from the image, spirited away during the operation.

During this time all three have remained motionless. X has a rather excited expression, A looks troubled, M is enigmatic. A few seconds after the oscillations stop, X speaks. A is evidently fascinated by his words.

X: *An arm is half bent toward the hair, the hand abandoned, palm open. . . . The other hand is resting on the chin, index finger extended, almost on the mouth, as though warning not to cry out. . . .*

Then, after a silence, X slowly turns toward A, stares at her and continues in a voice that is quite low and has difficulty maintaining its apparent neutrality.

X: *And now you are here again. . . . No, this isn't the right ending. . . . I must have you alive. . . . (A pause.) Alive . . . as you have already been, every evening, for weeks . . . for months . . .*

He stares at her intensely, as if he insisted on an answer. She turns toward him, seems for a moment on the point of yielding; then she imperceptibly shakes herself, as though waking from a dream, and it is with an almost harsh voice that she answers.

A: *I have never stayed so long anywhere.*

X: *Yes . . . I know. . . . I don't care. . . . For days, and days . . .*
(A pause. His voice a little weary:) *Why don't you still want to remember anything?*

A: *You're raving! . . . I'm tired . . . let me alone!*

The *You're raving!* is almost a scream of fear and hate combined. Then, suddenly, her two last phrases are blank, hopeless, abandoned. . . . She stands up at the same time. Then she slowly walks away. X makes no move to follow her. He merely watches her vanish in the perspective of columns and doorways. . . . The irritating and discontinuous music begins again on a few un-

certain notes, and develops during the shots that follow.

Close-up of X's face: excited at first, then growing milder with an unhappy smile, and finally freezing into a cold expression characteristic of him: hard, watchful but withdrawn, impenetrable.

Another shot of X, still in the same place, from a little farther away. Neutral face, eyes staring into space. He is resting one elbow on a low, round table that is close beside his chair. In his hand he has a box of matches, which he mechanically opens, watching the contents fall out onto the table. Little Italian matches; X watches them; begins to arrange them in the prescribed order: 7, 5, 3, 1, methodically but absently.

Transition dissolve: another table, with a set of dominoes spread out and a great many players around it (they are no doubt playing with several sets combined, to make more dominoes). The game is already far advanced, and a perfect labyrinth occupies the center of the table, a twisting path of futile complications. And the game continues: each player, in turn, placing a domino at the end or abstaining. X and M are among the players.

After various movements to show the game (it is the table that has been seen at first), then the players, a long lateral movement (perhaps a curve) of the camera begins, starting from the table. At first the part of the table where X is sitting, trying to place a domino, then his neighbors, one after the other, around to M, who is watchful and impassive (the same seriousness as in playing anything); then the camera, still in the same steady movement, abandons the table covered with dominoes; continues through the rest of the room, where there are other groups, playing or not; in the same way passes A standing motionless, against the light, in a window recess, first in profile, then looking outside; continues its same movement and (after other characters) comes back to X again, but alone and in another place altogether, perhaps even a little outside the room, in some passage (a hall or corridor) which is between the latter and another part of the hotel (another salon, a landing, etc.).

The camera still continues its movement, but it no longer meets anyone and soon comes up against a door (no doubt a rather monumental one, in any case it is not a room door, for there is no number on it).

The shot immediately changes, replaced by a new version of A's bedroom. There is now, aside from the setting and the furnishings—which have remained where they were the last time—a kind of proliferation of ornaments, either on the walls, or in the details of the furnishing: a considerable mass of added decoration, encumbering all the space with a stifling but realistic flood of embellishment.

The music has stopped with the new shot. Only the faintest sounds are now heard—also realistic, but perhaps slightly exaggerated by the sound track—of what is happening in the room: slippers flapping on the uncarpeted parts of the floor, a drawer opening, papers being shifted, etc. (Perhaps too, once or twice, sounds from outside, for instance a distant bell, a door closing, etc.; and each time, A listening intently, suddenly disturbed.)

It is night, the curtains are drawn. A is in her bedroom, wearing a white robe (over a nightgown, probably) that is extremely luxurious, gauzy, rather full; this must be both suitable and frivolous, and also in harmony with the excesses of the setting. A is standing in the middle of the room, looking both at home and a little lost. Her face is blank again, but this time it is no longer a polite blank, it is the blank of expectation. Eyes wide, hair brushed for the night but loose, lips made up, etc. This is a woman waiting for her lover or her husband rather than a woman about to go to sleep.

She takes a few uncertain steps, but not anxiously, as before, picks up a *bibelot* and looks at it, turns on a little lamp, approaches an open secretary-desk. All these gestures are a little dreamy, preceded and followed by long periods of waiting. She opens a drawer (not a little drawer, but something rather wide and deep) and rummages through it absently, finds a sheet of white paper (business size) and sets it on the writing surface. Looks in the drawer again, doesn't find what she is looking for (an envelope, a pencil?), rummages with both hands this time, opening the drawer wider, and thus reveals a mass of snapshots (postcard size or even larger). Not at all surprised to find them, A seizes a package of them, spreads them out on the writing surface: they are all photographs of A in the hotel garden, often in X's company; all come from scenes shown during the course of the film. A picks them up one by one and brings them close to her face to look at them better. Very distinctly (too distinctly, even?) the sound can be heard of the semi-stiff photographs she is manipulating.

The camera comes closer too, and the last photographs of the series appear in close-up, occupying almost the whole screen, and are no longer separated by A's gesture of setting down one image and taking up another. The change then occurs abruptly, the photographs remaining motionless. None the less the same sounds of manipulation are still heard.

The last image entirely fills the screen, without any margin, and could very well no longer be a photograph A is holding. It is only a stationary image. It represents X and A looking at the statue, and also comes from a scene shown at the beginning of the film. But the same sounds of the postcards being manipulated are heard again at the change in shot, and during the three following shots, although it no longer appears to involve photographs A might be examining.

Another stationary shot, continuing the rhythm of the sequence of photographs: the garden again, shown in a panoramic view. X and A are in the background, fairly small, seen from behind and, although motionless, seem to be moving away down a broad path seen in perspective. This view does not belong to a scene shown in the film.

View of another part of the empty garden. There is not a single person in sight. The image no doubt comes from a panoramic shot from the beginning of the film. The entire sequence of these images has gone by quite rapidly.

View of a game room in the hotel: the domino table as before, with almost all the players around it. But they are no longer playing dominoes. It is M's favorite game which is arranged on the table, this time with face-down dominoes set out in proper order: 7, 5, 3, 1. It is M and X who are about to play together, sitting opposite each other across the width of the oblong table (so that they have changed position). It is the table that is seen best, photographed from slightly above, as in the first images of the domino game.

After the sound of the photograph being manipulated, which marks the beginning of the scene, the commentaries made by the observers are immediately audible.

I think this game's silly.

There's a trick you have to know.

All you have to do is take an uneven number.

There must be rules.

It's the one who goes first who loses.

I remember how Frank used to play this, last year. . . . Yes, yes he did, I'm sure of it.

What you have to do is take the complement of seven each time.

In which row?

Having considered the table a long time, X signals that he is going to begin; the others all stop talking and X speaks, addressing M.

X: *I'd like you to begin.*

M: *With pleasure. . . . Which would you like me to take?*

X looks at M as though to see if he is being serious, then looks again at the table and points to the last domino in the row of seven (this is the row nearest M, the single domino being near X).

X: *This one.*

M: *Fine.*

Then M takes one from the row of seven, X takes two from the row of five, M takes five from the row of seven, X reflects for a second and takes two from the row of three, M takes the three remaining in the row of five. There then remain three isolated dominos. X stretches out his hand toward one of them and draws it back after a few seconds, without taking any, realizing that he has lost. The game has been rapid and silent.

X: *Well, I've lost.*

He slowly begins setting out the pieces for a new game, thinking about what he should have done, while the camera moves closer to him.

A slight hubbub of conversations develops, growing louder during a rather slow fade, and continues on the shot that follows. This is the bedroom again just as it was the last time: overly

elaborate furniture and decoration. A, in the same gown of white chiffon, is now sitting on the edge of the bed. All the photographs which she found in the desk are now spread all around her: on the bed, on the night table, on the carpet, in great disorder. Mingled with the images of the garden shown throughout the film at various points are also very obvious photographs of the scene that is going to take place in the room itself (with altered setting; see below). A is motionless, looking at the floor, and in particular at the images of what is going to follow (rape scene).

Against the confused background of mingled conversations, snatches of distinct phrases stand out here and there:

It's the one who starts who wins.
You have to take an even number.
The lowest whole uneven number.
It's a logarithmic series.

You have to pick a different row each time.
Divided by three.
Seven times seven forty-nine.

Sudden change of shot: X mounting a hotel staircase, monumental and empty. He is climbing slowly, using the middle of the steps. The silence is complete, as in the three shots that follow.

And then comes the bedroom again, but as it was before the proliferation of the ornaments: all the supplementary accessories have vanished, as have the photographs spread around on the furniture. A is in exactly the same position, looking at the floor, sitting on the bed, her arms slightly spread. She is dressed in the same way: a gauzy white robe. The shot is stationary; A is not shown directly, but in the mirror over the chest, the camera being quite far from this mirror. After a few seconds, A looks up toward the mirror, her eyes fixed on the camera through the mirror. Her face is suddenly agonized.

The shot immediately changes: A is still in the same position and setting, but not seen in the mirror, rather from the door, and turned toward this door, staring directly at the camera with a face overcome (by terror or by what?). Rapid shot.

This time the shot is taken from very close. Same setting. A is in the same position, staring at the camera which is now directly in front of her. A raises her arms half way, in a gesture of uncertain defense.

X appears in the foreground, seen from behind. Rather swift and brutal rape scene. A is tipped back, X is holding her wrists (in one hand) below her waist and a little to one side, her upper body thus not lying flat. A struggles, but without any result. She opens her mouth as though to scream; but X, leaning over her, immediately gags her with a piece of fine lingerie he was holding in his other hand. X's gestures are precise and rather slow, A's chaotic: she turns her head once or twice to the right and left, then stares again, her eyes wide, at X who is leaning a little farther over her. . . . The victim's hair is loose and her clothes in disarray.

Fade. A long, deserted corridor down which the camera advances quite rapidly. The lighting is strange: very weak on the whole, with certain lines and details violently emphasized.

Long labyrinthine trajectory—continuous or at least giving the

146

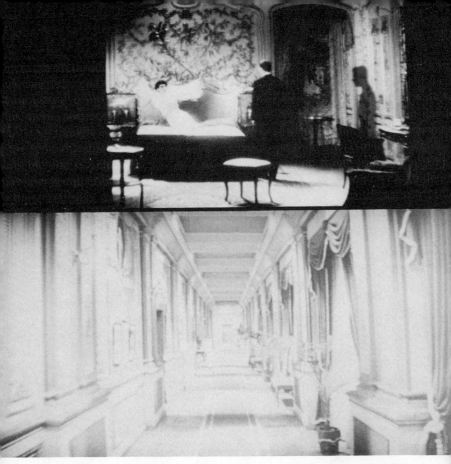

impression of continuity. Same darkness, same effects of light. There is no one left in the entire hotel. (Perhaps a brief fragment should be introduced of the long gallery that begins the film, this time ending with the empty theater, an empty stage, rows of empty armchairs, etc.) X's voice has resumed, from the beginning of the shot, offscreen.

X's VOICE: *No, no, no!* (violently:) *That's wrong. . . .* (calmer:) *It wasn't by force. . . . Remember . . . For days and days, every night . . . All the rooms look alike. . . . But that room, for me, didn't look like any other. . . . There were no more doors, no more corridors, no more hotel, no more garden. . . . There wasn't even a garden any more.*

147

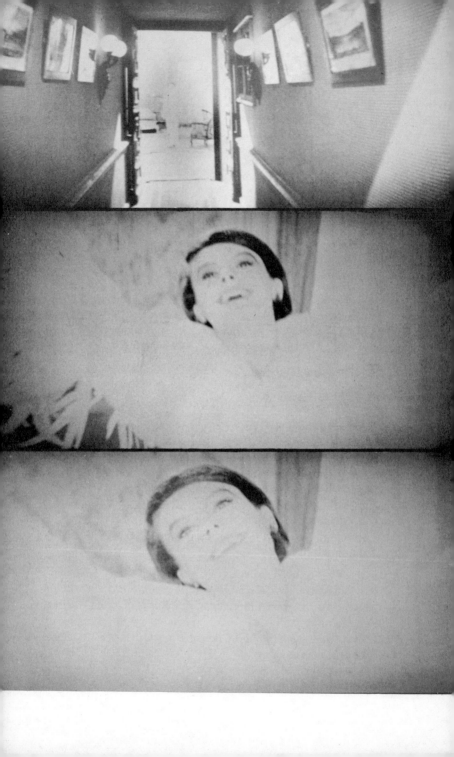

Finally the camera comes out onto the garden at night, and continues through it in the same way. Advancing along a broad, straight path, the camera reaches X, who is standing at the end of this path, shown in profile, perhaps leaning against the pedestal of a statue.

The camera stops when X is clearly visible: in the foreground, on one side of the screen and staring at the other. But the forward movement having stopped, the camera makes a quarter turn in the direction X is looking. X then leaves the field of vision, while A appears in it, but in the background. The image focuses on her: a silhouette surrounded in darkness, standing motionless staring fixedly at the camera.

After a long silence, the offscreen voice starts again, quite calm, having recovered its narrative tone, but noticeably more moved:

X's VOICE: *In the middle of the night . . . everything was asleep in the hotel . . . we met in the park . . . the way we used to.* (A pause.) *When you recognized me, you stopped. . . . We stood like that, a few yards from each other, without saying a word. . . . You were standing in front of me, waiting, unable to take a step or turn back either.* (A pause.) *You stood there, straight, motionless, your arms alongside your body, wrapped in some kind of long dark cape . . . maybe black.*

Slow fade during which the characteristic sound is heard of two people walking across gravel. And X and A are seen, closer together now in the same garden by night, but in another part of it: against a stone balustrade overlooking a considerable drop in ground level. (Perhaps the balustrade is obviously in bad condition, with a broken statue nearby?)

They are talking in low, clear voices. A is still wearing her long black cape, but it is parted to show the white nightgown. X looks harder, almost contemptuous. A is beside herself, hysterical, wringing her hands.

A: *Oh! Listen to me . . . for pity's sake . . .*

X: *We can't turn back now.*

A: *No, no. All I'm asking is that you wait a little. Next year, here, the same day, at the same hour. . . . And I'll come with you, wherever you want.*

X: *Why wait, at this point?*

A: *Please. I have to. A year isn't long. . . .*

X: (gently): *No . . . For me, it's nothing.*

The shot changes abruptly on the last word. . . . In a secluded corner of a salon in the hotel, X and A are shown in virtually the same postures as in the preceding shot, but both dressed normally. X's tone is the same, but a little wearier, grimmer. A's tone is less suppliant, more meditative, but perhaps more dramatic, though less spectacular. The set is characteristic of the entire hotel, but not too overdone, rather simple in its lines, almost austere compared with certain places shown previously.

A: *But, listen . . .*

X: *Then you need more time. Until when? Until when?*

A: *But, you see . . . I'm explaining it to you.*

X: *I've already waited too long.*

A: *Oh, don't talk so loud, please!*

X: *Whose feelings are we sparing? What are we protecting? What is it you're still expecting to happen?*

Silence, then A, in a very low voice:

A: *Do you think it's so easy?*

X: *I don't know.*

A: *And besides . . . maybe I don't have much courage.*

Silence.

X: *I can't put it off again.*

A: *No, of course not. . . . A few hours is all I'm asking you for.*

X: *A few months, a few hours, a few minutes.* (A pause.) *A few seconds more . . . as if you were still hesitating before separating from him . . . from yourself . . . as if his silhouette . . .*

X's last phrase is spoken in a voice that has grown a little remote, as though neutralized by distance and dreaming. As a matter of fact, it reproduces exactly the tone of this same phrase already heard offscreen at the beginning of the film (ideally, the same sound track would be used).

A (interrupting him): *Someone's coming! Be still . . . for pity's sake!*

The characteristic and close sound is heard of heavy footsteps on gravel. Fast fade on A moving away from X.

A's movement resumes on the following shot: she was beside X, even pressed quite close to him, and now quickly steps away, several steps back, murmuring vehemently that he should go away. The setting is again that of the garden by night: they are standing against a stone balustrade at the same point as in the shot before last, and in the same costumes.

A: *Go away . . . if you love me!*

Having stepped back, she looks toward the side of the screen where the footsteps seem to be coming from, repeated now, farther away but coming closer. X, without too much haste, with a kind of casual nonchalance, steps over the balustrade behind him, while holding onto the stone rail, and thus passes to the side where there is no ground behind him. But the movement is barely begun when the shot is abruptly cut.

A is seen full face close-up: worried expression, her eyes trying to pierce the darkness, but already sure of what will appear. Frozen anguish. The black cape slips from her shoulders without her making a gesture to hold it back. The sound of footsteps across the gravel comes closer and closer, then stops.

Reverse angle: M, standing, staring straight at the camera, a few yards away. He is motionless, in a posture seen several times during the course of the film: arms folded or something of the kind. He has a vague, enigmatic smile on his face. He doesn't react at the sound of the balustrade collapsing: a long roar of a considerable mass of big stones falling from quite a height onto a hard surface (a lower terrace, located several yards below). The shot is cut at the end of the collapse.

Another view of the stone balustrade from the angle at which it was seen before, or just about. A is in the foreground, seen from behind or almost, and staring at the collapsed balustrade: X has vanished, three or four balusters have disappeared, another is lying in front, the rail has crumbled too (on one side or the other) for about four and a half to six feet. The shot is entirely silent.

Reverse angle: A seen full face (close-up of her face or of her whole body in her white nightgown, with the black cape at her feet). Same frozen anguish as before. Then her mouth gradually opens and begins to scream: a long violent scream, either of terror or to break out of a spell.

Abrupt change of shot: a salon in the hotel, the ballroom for instance, near the bar, at the place where the scene of the broken glass occurred. A large crowd, probably couples who were dancing or taking refreshments . . . but everyone is motionless, facing A who has just screamed: this time the scandal is enormous, whereas the broken glass was only a minor incident. No one moves, the faces indicate surprise, anxiety as to what will happen next, fascinated interest under the mask of polite respectability. A is also frozen to the spot, her eyes enormous with anguish and a general expression of madness (without grimaces); her posture must be the same as in the preceding shot, but she is now in evening dress. X, in the same evening clothes as in the preceding garden scenes, is leaning on the bar with a kind of rigid casualness; he is looking

153

at A with a vague, hard look; he is quite close to her (it is no doubt to escape his words that she screamed, a moment before), but other people are also close enough so that it is not evident that X and A were together. A woman takes a step toward A, but evidently does not know what to do for her and seems afraid to come any closer. Other slight movements are made here and there. The scene lasts a long time in relation to the rapid shots that have preceded it. No one dares speak, or perhaps there are brief conversations in low voices. A *maitre d'hotel* touches A's arm respectfully; she looks at him blankly.

Another man approaches, coming from more remote regions: it is M. He says nothing either; without a glance at anyone, he takes a glass which a bartender hands him, stops in front of A and gives her the glass, standing very close to her; she takes it mechanically and drinks a few sips; she seems to be gradually waking from a dream. She hands the glass back to M, who passes it on and someone else hands it back to the bartender.

This scene includes all the usual sounds that are actually heard. Total silence must be avoided, for it would give the scene an unreal quality. And yet it is silence that reigns in the salon; but discreet sounds can be introduced—of glasses at the bar, of chairs being shifted in the invisible orchestra, of whisperings, of footsteps (there is no carpet, since this is the ballroom), all very distinct though of low volume. Then gradually the noises of conversation grow louder, while M exchanges a few phrases with A, he in a natural tone, she in a faint voice.

M: *An attack of indigestion, probably . . . A dizzy spell.*

A: *Yes . . . it's nothing.*

M: *You feel better already.*

A: *Yes . . .* (A pause.) *I'm going upstairs.*

M: *Would you like me to come with you?*

A: *No . . . Thank you . . . I'd rather be alone. . . .* (A pause, then as if speaking to herself:) *I'm leaving. . . .*

The shot is cut immediately, as she begins to leave the room.

A is shown from behind, hurrying down an empty corridor. She is in the same outfit as in the preceding scene. She is holding her long dress up to be able to walk faster. Rather long, silent, stationary shot (but with a few realistic noises).

X is shown walking slowly down the same corridor (or gallery) and in the same direction as A in the preceding shot. But he is seen full face, and the shot is not stationary: slow reverse traveling shot that keeps X at a constant distance. His expression is absent, his eyes empty. Some silence with a few faint sounds.

Same slow and steady camera movement, but as though in the opposite direction: the empty corridors (neither X nor anyone else) passing regularly in a forward traveling shot.

With this shot X's voice resumes offscreen, calm and deep, continuing on the following shots and during the transitions between shots.

X's voice: *And once again I was walking on down these same corridors, walking for days, for months, for years, to meet you. . . . There would be no possible stopping place between these walls, no rest. . . .* (A pause.) *I will leave tonight . . . taking you away with me. . . .*

Fade to a stationary view of the salon; M is alone, standing, lost in his thoughts, perhaps, but looking at some element of the setting.

X's VOICE: *It would be a year ago that this story began . . . that I would be waiting for you . . . that you would be waiting for me too. . . .* (A pause.)

Dissolve to A in her bedroom, brushing her hair. She is alone, sitting at her dressing table, in exactly the same position and clothes as when M came in before their long dialogue. The setting of the bedroom is also exactly the same.

X's VOICE: *A year . . . You wouldn't have been able to go on living among this trompe-l'oeil architecture, among these mirrors and these columns, among these doors always ajar, these staircases that are too long . . . in this bedroom always open. . . .*

It is night. A is quite calm. Her expression is merely lost. She is carefully, regularly brushing her hair. At one moment, she turns toward the dressing-room mirror and leans over to look at herself. . . .

The shot immediately changes: sudden appearance of the garden, in broad daylight. Stationary shot showing the debris of the balustrade lying at the foot of a high stone wall. Perhaps nearby there is the beginning of an ascending staircase. Sunshine.

Abrupt return to the bedroom: A is standing near the window, in front of the closed curtains. She lets a fold of the curtain she had raised fall back. Soft, heavy movement of the fabric. The bedroom is the same as when seen last. A moves about, examining the things around her attentively.

Then she lies down on her bed, not across it, as during the rape scene, but in a normal fashion, her bust slightly raised by the

bolster and the pillows at the head of the bed; her hair that she has carefully brushed spreads around her face on the pillow. Her pose is rather languid and seductive, without stiffness, her expression tormented but beautiful, and remote at the same time.

M comes in (no knock has been heard, but he is suddenly there, quite naturally, introduced perhaps by a camera movement) and he walks toward the bed. He stares at A in silence for several seconds before speaking.

M (sad, dreamy): *Where are you . . . my lost love . . .*

A (uncertain): *Here . . . I'm here . . . I'm with you, in this room.*

M (gently): *No, even that's not true any more.*

A (more urgent): *Help me, please, help me! Give me your hand. . . . Take my hands and hold them tight. . . . Hold me against you.*

M (makes a gesture toward her, but lets her arm fall back): *Where are you? What are you doing?*

A (with a cry that is scarcely contained): *Don't let me go.*

M (with emotion, but simplicity): *You know it's too late. Tomorrow I'll be alone. I'll walk through the door of your bed-*

room. It will be empty . . . (He moves a little away from the bed.)

A (desperately): *No . . . I'm cold. . . . No! Don't leave yet!*

M (simply): *But you're the one who's leaving, you know you are.*

But only a very small part of this dialogue is heard, half drowned out by X's offscreen voice which has resumed, from the first lines, as though to impose on A a less dramatic version of the scene, in which only ordinary and everyday things are supposed to have happened; it is her own words which X claims to report:

X's VOICE: *Yes, you felt better . . . yes, you're going to sleep now. . . . Yes, you'll be perfectly well by the time that Acker-son . . . or Paterson comes, the man you're supposed to lunch with tomorrow. . . . No, you don't need anything. . . . You don't know what came over you just now, in the ballroom. . . . You don't even remember very clearly what it was that happened. . . . You hope you didn't cause too much of a scandal, scream-ing like that.*

But before separating, A and M exchange a look that probably expresses despair. M leaves as discreetly as he came; A cannot help half sitting up on her bed to follow him with her eyes. Then she lets herself gradually fall back. After a silence, X's voice, offscreen, continues more rapidly:

X's VOICE: *Once the man left who is perhaps your husband, whom perhaps you love, whom perhaps you are going to leave to-night forever, without his knowing it yet, you packed a few things and prepared what you needed for a quick change of clothes.*

But on the screen, A makes no move to get out of bed.

Fade to a table of domino players. Neither X nor M nor A figures among them. The game is rather gay, but always polite. The laby-rinthine path of the dominoes already played is even more com-plicated than the first time, actually quite mad, given the custom-ary rules. The offscreen voice continues from one shot to the other:

X's VOICE: *It was arranged that we would leave during the night. But you had wanted to give one more chance to the man who still kept you back, it seemed. . . . I don't know. . . . I agreed.*

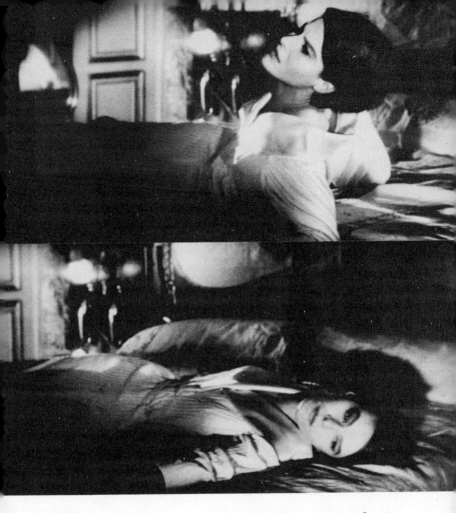

He should have come. . . . He could have come to take you back . . .

Dissolve to the stage of the little theater, as at the beginning of the film, with the same actor and the same actress on stage. But this is near the beginning of the play, and the setting is no longer the same: a salon or something of that kind. They are acting a scene whose words cannot be understood: the movement of the lips is shown, but no sounds are heard. Perhaps it is one of the early scenes between X and A? Or else from some standard play (Marivaux, etc.).

159

X's VOICE: *... The hotel was empty, as if abandoned. Everyone was at the performance, announced so long ago, from which your attack had excused you. ... I think it was ... I don't remember the title any more. ... The play wouldn't be ending until late at night. ... (A pause.) After having left you, lying on the bed in your room ...*

Fade (the speech still continues) to a moving shot which is the exact reproduction of a rather long fragment of the first sequence of the film: slow advance of the camera down the empty gallery toward the theater.

X's VOICE: *... he had headed toward the little theater where he had taken a seat among a group of friends. He would have to come back before the performance was over if he really wanted to keep you.*

Dissolve to A, alone now, waiting in a vague salon or passageway (where no one passes, anyway). A's costume is quite different from anything she has worn during the film: a kind of traveling suit, elegant and rather severe, perhaps quite dark. A is sitting on the edge of a couch. She looks as if she were waiting in the dentist's office or were at a railroad station between two trains. Now and then she looks at a baroque clock that ornaments the room (on the mantlepiece perhaps) an object of enormous size, decorated with bronze figures, very turn-of-the-century in style. The entire setting should be very ornate, and the labyrinthine architecture (mirrors, columns, etc.) characteristic of the hotel. A looks for something in her bag, finds a letter she begins reading (perhaps

160

she has written it); then she tears it into sixteen pieces (four times) and drops the pieces on the table (a long, low table in front of the couch), mechanically. Mechanically too, she begins arranging the bits of paper according to the classical figure of M's favorite game: 7, 5 . . . but before she has finished, she stirs up all the bits with a sudden gesture. Then she gathers up the bits of paper, tears them across again, looks for a place to put them and finally abandons them in an ash tray.

X's VOICE: *. . . You dressed to leave, and you began to wait for him, alone, in a kind of hall or salon, that had to be crossed to reach your apartment. . . . Out of some superstition, you had asked me to leave you there until midnight. . . . I don't know if you hoped for him to come or not. I even thought, for a moment, that you had told him everything and arranged a time when he would meet you. . . . Or else you were only thinking that maybe I wouldn't come myself.*

Then the offscreen voice continues, after an emphatic silence.

X's VOICE: *I came at the time we set.*

At this very moment, X appears. A looks at him, her face still blank. Had she hoped for the other man to come? X has stopped in the doorway (is there, over it, a full-length portrait of a man who greatly resembles M?). X himself looks tired, rather sinister. A looks at the face of the clock: there is still a two or three minutes' respite. A remains seated, her face blank, almost tense, her eyes lowered toward the table. X takes a few steps toward her. They say nothing to each other, even avoid looking at each other. She is still

161

seated, he is standing nearby. They do not look hesitant, but resolute, although at the end of their strength. X is in an elegant but not formal suit (for traveling).

A is staring at the clock when the first stroke of midnight sounds, making exactly the same sound as at the end of the play, at the beginning of the film. A doesn't move, and only at the second stroke does she stand up, like an automaton. She picks up her bag and begins walking, stiff and expressionless. X follows at a certain distance, with a gait that is just as tense. It is as if she were a distinguished prisoner and he the guard leading her away. The image disappears before they exit, while the strokes of the clock continue one after the other.

Fade: the same room, from the same angle (view taken toward the door through which X has come). The door is still open and looks down the galleries, etc. The room is empty.

After a moment, M appears in the background and walks toward this door. He stops a second in the doorway. He too looks exhausted, vague, ghostly, but more noticeably anxious. He continues walking straight ahead, looks absently at the ash tray with the bits of paper in it. He continues with the same slow steps. The clock chimes the first stroke of midnight. He turns around to glance vaguely at its face: it is five after twelve (it is a clock that chimes twice: on the hour, then at five past). He walks on toward his apartment. (The salon-hall might have three quite different exits: the one that leads to M and A's apartment, the one at the other end through which X and then M come, and finally the one through which X and A walk to leave the hotel.)

Slow fade. Then slow reverse traveling shot: the garden, by night, with a long, straight path, and at the far end, the façade of the hotel in moonlight. This same setting has already been seen, by day, with A advancing down the path. Now the entire setting is empty, and the camera moves back while the hotel, farther and farther away, seems none the less to grow larger and larger.

The serial music has begun again on the clock's second stroke (it is not necessary, either this time or the first, for all twelve strokes to be heard); the music continues on this shot, mingled now with X's offscreen voice, again slow and sure.

X's VOICE: *The park of this hotel was a kind of garden à la française without any trees or flowers, without any foliage. . . . Gravel, stone, marble and straight lines marked out rigid spaces, surfaces without mystery. It seemed, at first glance, impossible to get lost here . . . at first glance . . . down straight paths, between the statues with frozen gestures and the granite slabs, where you were now already getting lost, forever, in the calm night, alone with me.*

Afterwards the music rises and prevails.

165

Major Films by Alain Resnais*

1948: VAN GOGH. Conception: Robert Hessens and Gaston
Diehl. Direction: Alain Resnais. Music: Jacques Besse. Narrator: Claude Dauphin; (U.S. version: Martin Gabel). Production: Pierre Braunberger. Length: 22 minutes. Academy
Award, 1949.

1950: GAUGUIN. Conception: Gaston Diehl. Direction: Alain
Resnais. Text: Paul Gauguin. Music: Darius Milhaud. Narra-
tor: Jean Servais; (U.S. version: Martin Gabel). Special
Effects: Henry Ferrand. Production: Pierre Braunberger.
Length: 11 minutes. Shared the Grand Prize for short films at
the Punte del Este Festival, 1952.

1950: GUERNICA. Conception: Robert Hessens. Direction: Alain
Resnais and Robert Hessens. Cameramen: Ferrand and
Dumaître. Text: Paul Eluard. Music: Guy Bernard. Narrator:
Maria Casarès; (U.S. version: Eva La Gallienne). Production:
Pierre Braunberger. Length: 12 minutes. Shared Grand Prize,
Punte del Este, 1952.

1951: LES STATUES MEURENT AUSSI. Direction: Alain Resnais, Chris Marker and Ghislain Cloquet. Cameraman: Ghislain Cloquet. Text: Chris Marker. Music: Guy Bernard.
Narrator: Jean Negroni. Production: André Tadié; commissioned by the "Présence Africaine." Length: 29 minutes. Jean
Vigo Prize, 1954. Banned by the censors from 1954 to 1961;
then released in mutilated form.

1955: NUIT ET BROUILLARD (NIGHT AND FOG). Direc-
tion: Alain Resnais. Cameraman: Ghislain Cloquet. Text: Jean
Cayrol. Historical Advisors: André Michel and Olga Wormser.
Music: Hanns Eisler. Narrator: Michel Bouquet. Sound Edi-

---

*Further information on the work of Alain Resnais, a composite interview
with him, and the complete text of *Night and Fog* will be published by
Grove Press in *Film: Book 2: Films of Peace and War*, edited by Robert
Hughes.

tors: Henri Colpi and Jasmine Chasney. Color: Eastmancolor. Production: Argos Films and Como Films; commissioned by the Committee for the History of World War II Deportation. Length: 29 minutes. Jean Vigo Prize, 1956.

1956: TOUTE LA MEMOIRE DU MONDE. Conception: Remo Forlani. Direction: Alain Resnais. Cameraman: Ghislain Cloquet. Music: Maurice Jarre. Narrator: Jacques Dumesnil. Production: Pierre Braunberger; commissioned by the French Ministry of Foreign Affairs. Length: 22 minutes. Commission Supérieure du Cinéma Prize, 1957.

1958: LE CHANT DU STYRENE. Direction: Alain Resnais. Cameraman: Sacha Vierny. Text: Raymond Queneau. Music: Pierre Barbaud. Narrator: Pierre Dux. Color: Eastmancolor. CinemaScope. Production: Pierre Braunberger; commissioned by the plastics firm Péchiney. Length: 17 minutes. Golden Mercury Award, Venice Festival, 1958.

1959: HIROSHIMA MON AMOUR. (See Evergreen Original E284.) Two special jury prizes, Cannes 1959; and shared (with *The 400 Blows*) the Louis Méliès Prize, 1960.

1961: L'ANNEE DERNIERE A MARIENBAD (LAST YEAR AT MARIENBAD).